OTTO PENZLER PRESENTS
AMERICAN MYSTERY CLASSICS

# THE BIRTHDAY MURDER

LANGE LEWIS (1915-2003) was the nom de plume of Oakland, California, native Jane de Lange Lewis. A working writer throughout her life, Lewis only spent a decade working in mystery fiction, publishing six novels in the genre—five of which featured series character Richard Tuck—between the years 1942 and 1952. She also published under the names Jane Beynon and Jane Lewis Brandt.

RANDAL S. BRANDT is a librarian at the University of California, Berkeley, where he catalogs rare books and is the curator of the Bancroft Library's California Detective Fiction Collection. He lives in Berkeley, on the same street and just a block away from Lange Lewis's childhood home.

# THE BIRTHDAY MURDER

### LANGE LEWIS

*Introduction by*
### RANDAL S. BRANDT

### AMERICAN MYSTERY CLASSICS

*Penzler Publishers*
*New York*

Published in 2023 by Penzler Publishers
58 Warren Street, New York, NY 10007
penzlerpublishers.com

Distributed by W. W. Norton

Cover image: Andy Ross
Cover design: Mauricio Diaz

Paperback ISBN 978-1-61316-432-7
Hardcover ISBN 978-1-61316-431-0
eBook ISBN 978-1-61316-433-4

Library of Congress Control Number: 2023902479

Printed in the United States of America

9 8 7 6 5 4 3 2 1

# INTRODUCTION

"Almost perfect in its playlike purity and delightful prose."
—Barzun and Taylor on *The Birthday Murder*

LANGE LEWIS was a woman of mystery.

She made a splash in 1942 with the publication of her first novel, *Murder Among Friends*. It was praised in reviews published in the *New York Times* ("This appears to be Lange Lewis's first book. Let us have more"), the *San Francisco Chronicle* ("Salaams to Miss Lewis and a recommendation to any and all fans who like their detective stories literate, civilized, and well-planned"), and the *Oakland Tribune* ("Devotees of violent demise in literary form have a treat coming at the hands of this young woman, Lange Lewis"). The *Chronicle* and *Tribune* also ran a prominent headshot of the author. The photo shows a young woman with a stylish 1940s pompadour and contemplative eyes. Despite this early author's photo, for the most part, she eschewed author profiles both on her book jackets and in the press. Perhaps this is due to the fact that Lange Lewis led a fascinating and complicated life that did not lend itself to a brief summary.

Lange Lewis is the nom de plume of Jane de Lange Lewis, who was born September 10, 1915 in Oakland, California. Her parents, both artists, met when they were living in the same boarding house in Manhattan. Arthur Munroe Lewis and Jean ("Jennie") Clark de Lange were 40 and 41 years old, respectively, when they married in 1911. They then moved to Oakland, Arthur's hometown, where Jane was born. Arthur, who had previously been employed in the art department of the *San Francisco Chronicle*, found work as a magazine illustrator, and Jane's early childhood was spent in Oakland and Berkeley. In the 1920s, after a brief residence in Los Angeles, they moved back to New York where Arthur continued his career as a marine painter.

The Lewis family's time in New York was short, however. After Arthur's death in 1931 at age 59, Jane and her mother moved back to Los Angeles. Jane enrolled in Los Angeles High School and graduated in 1935. While in school, she was a member of the Poetry Club (her first known published writing was a poem in her senior yearbook) and the Philomathian Society. She then entered the University of Southern California as part of the Class of 1939, where she was a member of the Women's Literary Society and earned Phi Beta Kappa honors. She worked as a sales clerk and a bank teller to help support her mother.

On October 17, 1940, Jane married a twenty-three year old newspaper artist named William Mansfield Beynon. The day before the wedding William had registered for the draft and he was called up in November 1942, just months after Jane's debut novel was published. The marriage did not survive the war. What exactly happened to this young couple is unknown. Jane continued to use her married name until at least March 1944 when her fourth book, *Cypress Man*, appeared (under the name Jane Beynon). Not long after that she married her second husband.

Malcolm ("Mal") Havens Bissell, Jr., was the son of a prominent geographer, geologist, and humanist. Mal's father, after earning a Ph.D. from Yale, taught at Bryn Mawr College before heading west to Los Angeles to establish the Department of Geography at USC. Not destined to follow in his father's academic footsteps, young Mal wandered about Latin America working as a reporter and photographer for the Associated Press. It is not clear how Jane and Mal met, but after separating from her first husband Jane was living in an apartment near the USC campus, where she was working as a departmental secretary. Mal had returned home to Los Angeles and was living with his parents. It seems highly likely that they came into contact with one another somewhere on or near campus.

In 1943, Mal enlisted in the Army and in 1944, Jane and Mal (an aspiring writer himself) were married at Fort Ord in Monterey County. While he was in basic training, they collaborated on a mystery story, "Murder in Acapulco," which was published in the second issue of *Avon Detective Mysteries* in 1947 and is clearly inspired by Mal's Latin American adventures (the plot involves an American journalist, on his way from Mexico City to Buenos Aires, who gets involved in a murder on the Mexican Riviera). Their daughter, Haven Jean

Bissell, was born on February 6, 1945. Mal's military career ended in October 1945 after a lengthy illness resulted in his discharge. This marriage also did not survive and Jane and Mal divorced in 1948.

In 1952, Jane married again. On August 5, she wed George A. Brandt (no relation to this author) two months after the publication of her final mystery novel written as Lange Lewis. Shortly after their wedding they moved to Mexico City (perhaps Mal's tales of life south of the border made Jane want to experience it for herself), where she worked as a teacher at Colegio Coronet Hall from 1953 to 1959. After returning to California, Jane's third (and last) marriage also ended in divorce, in 1964, and she lived the rest of her life in the San Fernando Valley.

Lange Lewis's mystery-writing career lasted ten years, from 1942 to 1952, during which time she published six novels and one novella. All but *Cypress Man* and the novella she co-wrote with her then-husband Mal Bissell feature her series character, the tall (six feet five inches), phlegmatic, and methodical Lieutenant Richard Tuck of the Los Angeles Homicide Squad. The first three novels are set in and around a Los Angeles university.

Tuck investigates a group of medical school students following the death of a departmental secretary (*Murder Among Friends*, 1942), the murder of an aspiring actress playing the lead role in a drama department production of "Romeo and Juliet" (*Juliet Dies Twice*, 1943), and the poisoning of an eccentric vegetarian who has hired two recently-graduated English majors to help him write a stage play (*Meat for Murder*, 1943).

As an alumna of the University of Southern California, and then as a university employee after graduation, it is clear that Lewis wrote what she knew and set her stories there. In *Juliet Dies Twice*, Lewis attempts to disguise the campus by naming it "Southwest University," but eminent crime fiction critic Anthony Boucher (USC Class of 1932, who would have known) observed in his review that the book was "for USC alumni a grand roman à clef, for others that rarest of mysteries—a really good novel with a university setting."

For her fourth Tuck novel, *The Birthday Murders* (1945), Lewis leaves the academic setting behind and moves her narrative to the Hollywood movie colony where her protagonists, a successful novelist and her movie producer husband, live across the street from Humphrey Bogart. And, in her last book, *The Passionate Victims* (1952), Tuck re-opens a cold case involving the unsolved murder of a Hollywood High School freshman girl whose body had been found in Laurel Canyon six years before.

After the publication of the last Tuck novel, Jane curtailed her writing for a number of years. She published a few short stories, worked on a never-published novel, and edited a feminist newspaper called *Woman West* for six months until it folded in 1970. She made a comeback in 1975 with a historical romance set in Mexico titled *Love in the Hot-Eye Country*, published as a paperback original by Bantam Books.

For her new career as a historical novelist, she wrote under the name Jane Lewis Brandt. She had more success with her next historical novel, *La Chingada*, which reimagined the life of La Malinche, or Marina, a 16th century Nahua woman who served as an interpreter for the Spanish conquistador Hernán Cortés and was published in hardcover by McGraw-Hill in 1979. The novel was translated into Spanish, as *Malinche*, and both the English and Spanish editions were reprinted several times.

Jane Lewis Brandt died on February 1, 2003 at the age of 87.

Unfortunately, Lange Lewis is largely forgotten today. No movies were ever made from her books. Collectors of vintage "mapbacks" are likely familiar with the three Lewis titles published by Dell between 1944 and 1948. Book reviews were uniformly favorable.

Anthony Boucher thought *Meat for Murder* had "one of the year's most ingenious poisoning setups" and praised *The Birthday Murder* as "possibly the best of Miss Lewis' admirable novels." He speculated that 1944's *Cypress Man* may have been an early effort, "dug out of the trunk and somewhat revised," due to what he perceived as a 1930s sensibility among the characters. Although he was not as impressed with the plot as her other books, he nevertheless credited her "almost unique ability to write the kind of young people that I in those '30s knew and (I confess) was. I read her with interest, admiration and a certain mirror-conscious embarrassment." Boucher was disappointed with her last book, *The Passionate Victims*, which he thought was uneven. Although he did not publish a review, his notes on the book nevertheless praise the "beautiful detail work on middle-class L.A." and compare Lewis favorably to Margaret Millar,[1] who in four years would be named a Grand Master by Mystery Writers of America. Lenore Glen Offord, Boucher's successor as the mystery reviewer at the *San Francisco Chronicle*, however, gave it her second highest rating and called it a "well-written yarn" with detection theories that "make refreshingly good sense."

There appears to be critical consensus that *The Birthday Murder* ranks at the top of Lange Lewis's oeuvre. Barzun and Taylor included entries for four of her books in their landmark *A Catalogue of Crime* and had especially nice things to say about it: "There is no lost motion or verbiage. The author's sense of character is displayed, too: the book is full of women sharply differentiated . . . Almost perfect in its playlike purity and delightful prose."[2]

The mystery revolves around Victoria Jason Hime, a successful writer, and her recently-wed husband, Albert Hime, a producer of "Class B" films. Victoria's latest novel, *Ina Hart*, a story about a woman who poisons her husband, has been optioned by Hollywood and Albert is being considered to produce it (which would be his first "Class A" project). When Albert ends up murdered the night before Victoria's thirty-fifth birthday, in exactly the same manner depicted in *Ina Hart*, suspicion naturally falls on the widow. Lieutenant Tuck, who always seems to be the one called upon to investigate "when violent death left its usual haunts on the wrong side of the tracks and entered a home in Beverly Hills, a Los Angeles university

1     Anthony Boucher Book Review Card Files, BANC MSS 2012/179, The Bancroft Library, University of California, Berkeley.

2     Jacques Barzun and Wendell Hertig Taylor. *A Catalogue of Crime* (New York: Harper & Row, 1989), 346.

or other such genteel places," arrives on the scene and takes charge.

In all of Lange Lewis's stories characterization is at least equally as important as detection and in this novel the female characters stand out. Victoria Hime, her oldest friend Bernice Saxe, Moira Hastings, an ambitious young ingénue who covets the lead role in *Ina Hart*, and even Victoria's myopic and absent-minded maid Hazel, are all distinctly drawn and thoroughly developed. Lewis gives each of them plenty to do to keep the plot moving, and their attitudes towards things like work and marriage display a modern feminist sensibility.

Lange Lewis does miss a trick, however, in leaving one of her recurring female characters, Briget Estees, out of *The Birthday Murder*. Brigit is introduced in *Murder Among Friends* as the only woman on the Los Angeles Homicide Squad. And she is not in the squad room just to make coffee or type reports. She is a full-fledged, if junior, member of the team, actively participating in the investigation, bantering with Tuck and the other detectives, and offering her own opinions and insights into the case.

As Lewis describes her, Briget is five foot eleven, has red hair, wears size eight oxfords, and is a "hundred and fifty pounds of healthy womanhood." Together, she and Tuck make an imposing pair. She is about to take a larger role in the investigation when she is re-assigned to go undercover in another case in which a deadly stalker, dubbed "Black Overcoat" by the police, has already killed five women (spoiler alert: Briget gets her man).

After this promising start, however, Lewis dropped the

character from her second book, *Juliet Dies Twice*. Briget returned in the third book, *Meat for Murder*, and again played a small but significant role in the investigation before finally taking center stage in the last novel.

In *The Passionate Victims*, she is still the only woman in the Los Angeles Homicide Department, but Briget is now on an equal footing with Tuck. She chases down leads on her own, interviews suspects and witnesses, and even takes a bullet in the line of duty. Maybe with all of those other strong, well-developed female characters in *The Birthday Murder*, Lewis felt there was no room for one more. Had she included Briget in the Hime murder investigation, it could have provided a nice bridge from the character's relatively minor contribution in *Meat for Murder* to her major role in *The Passionate Victims*.

At the time Lange Lewis began writing, women had been working in the LAPD for over thirty years, so adding a female detective to her series seems like an obvious choice. In fact, with her first appearance coming in 1942, Briget Estees may just be the first female homicide investigator in an American crime novel. She is definitely in the vanguard. One cannot help but think, though, that Briget represents an opportunity missed and that had Lewis better-developed this aspect of her novels, she would have stood a much better chance at a higher profile among current mystery aficionados.

In a profile published in *Contemporary Authors* in 2002, the year before she died, Jane wrote:

"If I have any advice at all for young writers it is: Have another way than writing to feed your face and throw a bone to the wolf at the door, and learn to rewrite. No word you put on paper is immortal or carved in stone or engraved in bronze. A good way to cut is with scissors. Scotch tape is responsible for more good transitions than the typewriter. As for the question 'Should I be a writer?' the best answer still is 'Only if you can't help it.'"

Luckily for mystery fans, Jane de Lange Lewis Beynon Bissell Brandt couldn't help it.

—RANDAL S. BRANDT

# THE BIRTHDAY
# MURDER

*Chapter One:*
## ACTRESS ON THE MAKE

WHEN VICTORIA JASON married Albert Hime, her fifty most intimate acquaintances gasped. Some wondered how she got him. The majority wondered how he got her. The witty ones amused themselves by postulating, with delight, the number of bizarre situations which a marriage involving Victoria Jason might bring to full, rich flower.

For when the image of Victoria was called to their minds, it was Victoria in the throes of explaining a story she was writing. At such times she paced. If she happened (as was frequent) to be wearing slacks and a shirt, the shirttails always worked themselves out and ballooned behind her small solid body as she pursued a thought down the length of a room. Her short, crisp, graying hair, which looked at best as though it were being blown forward by a strong wind, was described by one dazed observer as having been stirred by an egg beater. Her harlequin eyeglasses became crooked on her pointed face; her cigarettes were stabbed out on any horizontal surface;

2 · LANGE LEWIS

she drank from a glass and set it down just short of the table, staring with startled but disinterested eyes as it fell to the floor and shattered. By the time Victoria came to consider her idea adequately explained, everyone present was limp with exhaustion; Victoria would peer triumphantly from face to face, her mouth stretched wide in its engaging smile, her gray eyes bright as a child's, quite unaware that she looked like a person who had just fled from a burning house.

And Albert was a quiet man.

But none of these speculations about the marriage approached the truth, which once more justified itself as being stranger than fiction. Nor did Victoria's own speculations. The worst Victoria could imagine was another divorce, excusable when it happened to Victoria Jason Harriss at 24, and even a little sad, but if it happened to Victoria Jason Hime at 34, minus the sanction of youth and ardor and hotheadedness, lugubrious and embarrassing failure. And Victoria did not like failures.

So it was not until six months after his first proposal of marriage that she agreed to marry Albert. Albert got Victoria. He got her because she liked him, because of his frank admiration of what he called her "story mind" and because of unfailing small attentions, pleasant to a woman who had for 15 years worked on equal terms with men. Albert treated her like a woman, and a desirable one.

Before she agreed to the marriage Victoria refused him flatly and took an unnecessary trip to New York, where she allowed herself the lachrymose indulgence of revisiting the scenes where her first marriage had spun to its ugly close.

When she returned to her little house in Beverly Hills, she found it full of Albert's flowers; a large, solemn and somehow touching box of Albert's chocolates bulked on the coffee table in the living-room, and an invitation to dinner with Albert was relayed by Victoria's devoted maid, Hazel, who opportunely remarked, "He certainly seems to care for you, dear."

Victoria retired to her room, wept briefly (she did not know why), and that night at dinner reversed her decision.

Albert Hime was a pleasant man. People liked, him, although never intensely. Smallish, neat, well-dressed, he chose only the most conservative checks and plaids, so that while his appearance suggested Southern California—Albert was a producer of Class B films—it did not suggest Hollywood at all. He had a smooth face which wore a moderate tan when he was not too busy at the studio for an hour's sun each day; otherwise it was pallid except at the day's end when his dark beard showed bluely against his skin. His eyes were almost dreamy, and were of a pale, melted-greenish color edged by dark lashes, topped by black brows. His ears had a peculiar attraction for Victoria. They were neat and pointed and showed at close range a faint, hirsute softness, like the bloom on a peach.

They dined at Chasen's; Albert was at home with its elegance. "A few years ago," he said, "I might have wanted to marry a quite different person. Now I want more than a pretty face with nothing behind it. I want an intelligent woman with whom I can talk and work and plan."

"It sounds," said Victoria, "very dull."

He shook his head, smiling a little. "The pretty women don't really give enough, Victoria. They take more from a man than they ever give back. You are not a pretty woman. You have one of the most interesting faces I have ever seen. I have often thought that your face would be good carved out of some smooth golden wood. The planes are excellent—strong, proud, and clean." He examined her face for a moment with his dreamy eyes. They met hers, and were infinitely kind and knowing. "You would always give a man a little more than he ever expected. You would give it and accept no thanks and say, 'Skip it, forget it, I'm glad I had what you needed of me.'"

Touched, Victoria did not want to show it. "In other words," she said lightly, "I'm a good deal."

Albert laughed delightedly. "Yes, if you want to put it that way, you are. But this is unimportant. You haven't told me yet what made you change your mind, what made you decide finally to marry me."

Victoria grinned at him. "I think it's because your name is Albert, 'Victoria and Albert.' It's more than I could resist."

Because he was producing a film, and because she had just signed a contract for a studio writing assignment, they were married quietly in the Los Angeles City Hall in the chambers of a white-haired judge, during his lunch hour. The next day a modest picture of them taking out the license appeared in a local paper. Albert, small, handsome, and assured, the flower in his buttonhole a trifle wilted; Victoria, staring with a smile of imbecile fascination at her own hand grasping a pen which looked as though it had been placed there hurriedly by someone else.

"Do I really look like that?" she asked Albert. It was the morning after their wedding. They were seated side by side on the sofa in the living-room of Victoria's house. Hazel was busy disposing of the last signs of revelry left from the enormous and casual reception of the night before.

"You're not photogenic," he told her. Glancing closely at him, she saw that he was looking at his own pictured face, not hers. This evidence of masculine vanity amused her.

"We're going to get on well," she said. "I think we understand each other."

"You do me too much credit," he told her with solemn amusement. "You are a riddle to me. I always feel that you see through me like glass, and just as I think I have you down pat, you do something to confuse me."

But in spite of this happy beginning, the first few months of their marriage were trying ones. Albert felt it somehow slighting to him that they should live in Victoria's house. It was a low adobe structure, the rooms sprawling around a small center patio, the tiled roof almost hidden by thick bougainvillea vine whose vivid cerise was all that could be seen through the low, close-packed trees of the deep front yard. For no known reason, the front door opened directly into the dining-room. The living-room, with its floor of big terracotta octagonal tiles, lay long and dim beyond it. This room was casually furnished with comfortable chairs, a sofa which had seen better days, vivid orange curtains. On either side of the fireplace at the far end were two packed bookcases. On the wall facing the south window three grotesque Mexican masks of tin stared down. There were two more of these in the dining-room. Victoria had made few changes since buying the house and its furniture. She had liked the place immediately, because it had seemed to her a house which did not try to be charming, or arresting, or anything but itself. She still liked it. Albert did not.

Victoria refused to rent the large Brentwood place he desired, pointing out that a larger house could not possibly be cared for by Hazel alone, while the employment problem would make the hiring of another servant impossible. And anyhow, she didn't want another servant. She had for several years enjoyed the comfortable arrangement of being cared for by Hazel, who knew all her little ways, and she did not want to change.

So Albert moved from his apartment at the Garden of Allah into Victoria's guest room. This was separated from her bedroom by the bathroom and her den. In the closet Albert's many expensive suits hung from polished hangers. A big English clothesbrush reposed on the highboy.

There was also the problem of Hazel's day off, Thursday. Albert wanted to dine out; Victoria did not like waiting for an hour in a crowded café for her dinner. This problem, too, was solved according to Victoria's preference. Before Hazel left on Wednesday night she prepared a casserole dish, and left a large undressed salad reposing beside it in the icebox. On Thursday, Victoria became domestic; toward evening she set the table, made coffee, heated rolls, put dressing on the salad and put the casserole in the oven, which she set at the proper temperature indicated in the note Hazel always left on top of the stove.

But the Thursday night casseroles and the loss of the Brentwood mansion were more than made up for in another way. Five months after their marriage Albert came home one night with the news that the studio was almost certainly going to let him produce his first Class A picture, the screen version of a book of Victoria's called *Ina Hart* which the studio had bought some time before. He told her, quite frankly, that this opportunity had come about because of *The Cold Boy*. He kissed her warmly on the lips and handed her a box of chocolates and a bunch of salmon pink gladioli. His eyes were once more full of the admiration they had worn in the days of his courtship.

*The Cold Boy* had shown no early signs of being more than a Class B horror picture. Albert had discussed it with Victoria months before their marriage. He was not satisfied with the script his writers had finally submitted, and asked her opinion. Victoria saw in the nuclear story possibilities for an unusual film. In one of her famous pacing fits she outlined to the rapt Albert an entirely new story line. He admitted its superiority but was fearful that Victoria's story was too unusual. Victoria loudly scorned the faithful belief that a mystery horror film must involve a gorilla which is really someone in disguise, a mummy with strongly gregarious impulses, or a fanged gentleman in a black opera cape who sucks blood from the throat of a young woman wearing a low-cut nightgown. She spurred Albert on to have his writers do a scenario along the lines she had outlined, prophesying that it would be the making of him. Albert summoned up the courage to follow her suggestions, and her prophecy came true. A month before their marriage *The Cold Boy* was previewed in Glendale, and the next day both *Variety* and *The Hollywood Reporter* were loud in their praise. Said the latter. *Tense, skillfully wrought melodrama rising out of the strange chaos of a twisted mind,* The Cold Boy *is by far the best mystery film of the year. Hime, although limited by a small budget, has managed to create out of what might have been a run-of-the-mill story something so unusual in its effects that it is actually Class A in quality. Although delving into the realm of abnormal psychology, the story is so gripping that we can confidently predict a box-office success.*

And five months after their marriage came this splendid news that the studio was considering him as producer of *Ina Hart.* Albert relegated Victoria's quirks and stubbornness to the realm of unimportance. He took to whistling while he shaved.

Albert was, for Victoria, the perfect husband. The intimate part of their marriage was by unspoken mutual agreement placed second to the work to which they had both for so long given first place. Albert was considerate, charming, and no bother at all. Victoria found her life with him far more to her liking than the marriage she remembered, for all the burning ardors of young love.

Only one thing troubled her. Whenever she found herself infrequently in Albert's room, it would seem to her that Albert had no permanent place in her life, that one day the suits would be gone from the closet, the clothesbrush from the highboy, and Albert would be gone too.

"Yes," said the young woman in gray who was standing beside the fireless hearth. "Yes," she repeated in a flat, tired voice, "I killed him." She moved slowly, hesitantly away from the fireplace, down the room, with an almost sidling motion. Her aquamarine eyes were wide, and about her small lovely face her tawny hair was disarrayed. Her voice became soft, wheedling. "You know it all, my dear. You know it all, don't you? And you can see, can't you, you can see that I had to kill him? Oh, you must see! There was nothing else I could do!" Her thin hands were out, imploring, while her curious light eyes probed to see the effect of hex words. She stood that way for a second, pitiful and watchful, and then she dropped her hands to her sides, and faced the gray-haired woman watching her from the corner of the sofa. She smiled and the older woman smiled back.

"Darling, it stinks," said Victoria, with no malice.

"Why?" asked Moira Hastings, bent over the coffee table where the tea things were laid out, to take a cigarette from the open red box. The hand holding the match trembled almost imperceptibly.

"You're a good actress but you haven't had enough experience to play Ina."

Moira Hastings sank into the low armchair facing the coffee table. She crossed one leg with an effect of nonchalance, but her eyes were far from casual. They were direct, cool, and filled with dislike.

Victoria said, "When Ina says, 'There was nothing else I could do!' you say it as though it were actually true. That's all wrong. Think of the sort of person who could say that about the fact that she has killed a man! She's a monster, Ina Hart is. All her life she has lived by using men; that has become the only way she knows. And then she comes against a situation where this old way fails her. There was only one way in which Jeffrey could aid her, and that was by dying. So he had to die. When she says, 'There was nothing else I could do!' she is telling the bitter truth, but she doesn't know this. You don't get this across in your reading of that final speech; you don't get it at all. You should be thinking of Jeffrey's dead sprawled body; you should be remembering how Ina gave him the poison in his medicine and smiled when she said, 'Drink this, dear!'"

"I see," said Moira Hastings, nodding, "but what of the rest of the scene?"

Decisively Victoria slapped shut the script which had lain open across her knees. She tossed it to the other end of the sofa. "The same thing. Not enough underneath. You're awfully good for your age, or rather your youth. But Ina isn't a part for a young actress. Give up the notion of doing Ina. It would be bad for the picture, bad for my husband as producer of the picture, bad for you, and bad for me. Have your agent get you another part like Clarissa. You were charming as Clarissa—no one could have done it better."

"I hated Clarissa; I don't want any more ingenue roles," said Moira Hastings quietly.

Victoria smiled at her. "I know. When I was your age I wanted to write deathless prose about sophisticated continentals who dropped bitter *bons mots* into each other's Martinis. I was very lucky. I met an editor who told me to do a story about a working girl and that was the first story I ever sold."

"I'll be typed; that damned Clarissa will type me," said Moira. "I want to prove my capabilities as a dramatic actress."

"Not on my story," said Victoria.

Moira tilted her head to one side and smiled very sweetly at

Victoria. "But you really have no authority as to the casting, do you?" she asked. "I mean, you sold the book to the studio and got paid for it and that sort of lets you out, doesn't it?"

"Except that my husband is going to produce it; don't forget that," said Victoria cheerfully.

"Oh, is that settled, then?" asked Moira Hastings. "I thought Mr. Leighman was still debating whether he wants Mr. Hime to do it or that other producer he's interested in."

"George always wavers for a week before he makes up his mind. He'll choose Albert, because Albert's the better man."

"I certainly hope he does. Your husband is very keen to do this film, Mrs. Hime. Your husband thinks I could handle the part. He's a very smart man. He was surprised when you told him I wasn't good enough. That's why I came up to see you, really. I hoped to convince you otherwise."

"I'd rather guessed that," said Victoria dryly.

"But what if Mr. Hime gets to do the picture and decides not to accept your opinion, Mrs. Hime?"

"Albert always accepts my opinion," said Victoria.

"What if Mr. Leighman likes me?" asked Moira. "After all, he'll be the executive producer. He'll have the final word on the casting, won't he?"

"Mr. Leighman," said Victoria inexorably, "has been a very good friend of mine for six years. When he was only a producer, we were a good team, he and I. He insists on believing that his success is partly due to some writing I did for him then. He has a faith in my opinion which is incredible."

"You seem to hold the cards, Mrs. Hime."

"You are sitting there hating my guts," said Victoria, "and

yet I've given you darned good advice. I'll admit that I've given it chiefly from selfish motives; I want *Ina Hart* to be good both for Albert's sake and my own. But it's still excellent advice. A few more parts like Clarissa to build you at the box office, and then try for something big. If this is any comfort to you, when that time comes Albert and I will go to bat for you in any way we can. How old are you?"

"The publicity department says I'm twenty-two. I'm really twenty-four, almost twenty-five."

"Tsk, tsk—so old you are," said Victoria.

"For an actress it's different! You're a writer, and you—" the younger woman's eyes assessed Victoria's fluff of graying hair, her dark blue slacks, her red play shoes with the bow missing from one of them—"you can look as old as you please."

"Tea?" asked Victoria, reaching out toward the urn which stood between them on the coffee table, flanked by the silver sugar bowl and a plate of pastries.

"Thanks, two cups is plenty, though."

"How about a drink?" Victoria hoped Moira would refuse. It was Hazel's day off and Victoria hated nothing more than manipulating ice trays.

"No, thanks, I don't drink. It's bad for the figure."

The telephone rang.

"Excuse me," Victoria said. The telephone was in the narrow hall opening off the dining-room, at right angles to the front door. Her business manager demanded in an outraged voice, "What is this check, five hundred dollars to the Red Cross?"

"Just what it says. They really wanted warm clothing, but I'd given all I had to China, so I sent money instead."

"Are you Rockefeller," he demanded rhetorically, "that you should be writing checks like that?"

Victoria heard the water running in the kitchen, whose door was across the dining-room from the hall. People were apt to make themselves at home in her house; it seemed to invite it and she never minded. Her business manager was saying, "Furthermore, what is this check for a hundred dollars to a Tina Geller?"

"She's a very old friend of mine; we worked together years ago in New York. She's temporarily broke."

"I give up, absolutely," snarled Ben. "I limit you here, I limit you there—and you break out somewhere else. Do you know what your income tax will be this year? Do you know you have had your dog spayed at a veterinarian who is charging you enough so he should be removing your appendix plus lifting your face at the price? Why should this dog be spayed anyhow?"

"She keeps having puppies and leaving them around the house."

"Puppies are salable."

"Not the puppies Haggis has. Being a bitch, she has no taste in men. And anyway, who makes this money, you or me?"

"You are making it, but are you keeping it? Or are you throwing it around like a drunken philanthropist? Suppose there is no screen sale for fifty thousand next year? What are you doing then?"

"I am buying a tambourine and dancing in the streets. And now I am hanging up."

When Victoria returned to the living-room, Moira was

slumped in the big chair again, her long and lovely legs stretched out comfortably, her hands with their, long nails clasped over her stomach. "What were you doing in the kitchen?" asked Victoria.

"I had to take my pill," Moira said. "Vitamins." She regarded Victoria steadily for a moment, her chin down against her breastbone, and then she jumped up with a nervous little laugh. "I must go now. Thanks for the tea—thanks so much!"

At the Mexican half-door the mellow light of late afternoon, softened by the trees which crowded about the house, struck both their faces: the young face, smooth and almost edible-looking in its peach-colored coat of make-up; the flat-cheeked tan of the older face. The pale aquamarine eyes, like jewels in the cross lighting, met the sparkling gray ones.

"Good-by," said Victoria, and put out her hand, which Moira Hastings, after a moment's hesitation, took in her own. But she drew away quickly and turned toward the door, the lower half of which Victoria swung open. Moira Hastings stepped out onto the porch with its hanging ollas, its faded bullfight poster plastered against one wall.

She turned smartly on her high heels and went down the steps to the driveway where her green topless car was parked. As the sunlight struck her hair it shone with a brassy and unreal luster, and her slim but shapely hips moved under the thin gleaming gray of her dress with a learned and ladylike voluptuousness. Walking away like that, her face not showing, Moira Hastings seemed to Victoria less real than fictitious; a figure standing in that moment for something minted by the hundred in this strange town, the young actresses, all so much alike in the cool drive of their ambition, differing only in the varying ways which served them to achieve what they wanted. Moira Hastings had selected perhaps the best way: a top-notch agent plus an up-and-coming producer with whom she might rise.

As Victoria turned back into her empty house she realized that the next day was her 35th birthday. Perhaps the vivid youth of Moira Hastings had brought the thought to the surface of her mind. She realized that this was the first birthday in many years for which she had not planned a party involving the two dozen most intimate of her friends. As an only child, her birthdays had been made much of; the rapture over unwrapping many mysterious packages was something she had never outgrown. But this year, for some reason, she had planned no party. She had been busy on a story, of course, but then that was nothing new. There had been Albert, and his gnawing anxiety as to whether or not he would get the chance to do *Ina Hart,* but that was after all his problem, and outside a natural concern had not deeply troubled her. *Perhaps,* she thought, *perhaps I'm just growing old.*

The thought was a melancholy one. Graying hair, a need to watch her diet to avoid unbeautiful hips, a deepening of the laugh lines around her eyes—these had not bothered Victoria. She always felt young, always felt as though most of her life lay ahead of her. But this year she had made nothing of her birthday, had almost forgotten it.

She had no way then of knowing that her 35th was to be the most memorable of all the birthdays of her life.

*Chapter Two:*

## A SHOULDER TO CRY ON

THE MINUTE she saw Bernice Saxe standing there in the doorway, she knew something was wrong, terribly wrong. Bernice Saxe was her oldest friend. They had known each other since they had been children of twelve, and although their lives had taken very different patterns, they had remained friends down the years. Bernice was a tall, pretty woman with a little-girl voice that contrasted oddly with her size. She spent a great deal of time and money on her clothes, which were always of the best. Her large face was beginning to show a tendency to sag around the jaw line; she used a pink net strap at night. She had very beautiful small feet and her shoes cost as much as many women spend on an entire outfit. Today she was wearing a handsome gray pin-striped suit which displayed her fine bustline to advantage. Over it was tossed a silver fox scarf, a Christmas gift from her husband, Walter. She was wearing no hat, and this was odd, for Bernice loved hats almost as much as shoes. Her shining chestnut hair, worn sleek and smart against her head, was very slightly disarrayed, and this too was unusual. But the oddest thing of all was the fact that Bernice was clutching a green lizard bag, although her shoes and gloves were black suede, and there was no touch of green elsewhere about her costume. She stood in the doorway with her shining brown eyes opened very wide, and Victoria had the feeling that at any moment she might topple over and crash to the tiled floor of the porch.

Victoria reached out and took Bernice's hand. Even through the black suede glove Bernice's hand seemed stiff and cold. Her fingers did not close on Victoria's, but remained in position. It was like holding the hand of a mannequin in a store window.

Bernice took three steps forward and then said, "I don't know what to do!"

Victoria led her into the narrow hall where the many bottles of an improvised bar stood in a deep window embrasure opposite the telephone niche.

"I'm going to get you a drink," she said.

"Walter's found out everything!" Bernice shrilled in her tiny voice. "There was a letter months ago that I lost and Stan's letters were always so affectionate and Walter found it, but I didn't know that. And then he began to notice things, and he had us followed by a private detective last week-end and today he made a scene and he is going to divorce me."

Victoria held out a small glass of whisky. Bernice looked down at it and said, "You know I can't stand straight whisky!" So Victoria added seltzer and then went to the kitchen, Bernice talking at her heels, where she wrestled ice out of the tray.

Bernice took the glass from her. Moisture on its side wet her suede glove but she did not notice that, and she drank thirstily, making little sucking noises like a child.

"Let's go into the living-room," Victoria said.

The ice tinkled in Bernice's glass as she followed, and her high heels clicked on the floor. She was silent for long enough to sit down on the sofa and finish her drink. She stared at the silver tea things, still on the low table. Then she burst out, "Walter was dreadful, cold and icy as though I was in the witness box. And he means it, Victoria! He means it! He'll do it! I'll have all the disgrace of his getting the divorce and not a cent of alimony!"

"Some husbands are apt to take infidelity hard."

"The things he said to me! Oh, no name-calling, but it was worse than that! And the slyness of it, suspecting it for so long and just biding his time."

"I imagine that the fact it was Stan annoyed him as much as anything else. Stan's so obviously a bounder, to use the term Walter probably used in speaking of him."

"Vicky! How did you know?"

"Well, try to figure it as the world well lost for love."

"But I can't! What would I live on!"

"It's not your fault," said Victoria. "It's your upbringing that's to blame."

"My mother was a *good woman*!"

"Yes. She was. She raised you to believe that your virginity should command the highest price in order to justify its existence. You married a man of thirty-eight when you were twenty. You didn't love him. Remember what she said when you got cold feet and told her you didn't want to go through with the wedding?"

"She said, 'But the invitations are all out,'" recalled Bernice.

"Yes. So you divorced him when you were twenty-seven. I don't particularly blame you for that. He'd had his money's worth. But—" What she was about to say congealed in her mouth. She couldn't say it.

Bernice's voice was bitter. "Oh, it's all very well for you to talk. You've had all the luck in the world on your side. I've always been unlucky," she said tragically, and twisting her body she buried her head in the sofa cushion and began to cry with rich self-pity.

"Oh, for God's sake," said Victoria. "You didn't have to do the same thing twice! You didn't love Walter either. After your first divorce you were young. You could have found work to do, made some sort of job for yourself. But you didn't. You went to Europe, and then when Herrick died with no money and the alimony was gone you were face to face with the problem of putting a roof over your head. Walter came along."

Bernice's long graceful body writhed on the sofa. "Stop it!" she said.

"All right. I'll stop." Victoria picked up Bernice's glass and took it to the bar. She mixed them both a drink and came back. Bernice was sitting up drying her eyes.

"We'll get along, Stan and I," she said. She reached for the glass Victoria held out. "I know you don't think much of him, but he's very sweet, and he'll stand by."

"You mean you're going to let Walter go through with the divorce and then marry Stan?"

"Obviously." Her cry after Victoria's unkindness seemed to have soothed Bernice. But her voice held the small edge of doubt. She extended one foot and looked closely at her black suede pump. She straightened the seam of her stocking. She seemed to be thinking; two lines showed between her eyes. "Obviously," she repeated, with an attempt at jauntiness.

Victoria hesitated, decided where the greatest friendship lay, and plunged. "He won't marry you."

The eyes Bernice raised to hers told her that Bernice had also thought of this. "Why do you say that?" she asked, carefully.

"Stan's happy as he is, being supported by his mother. He's a mother's boy. He'll tell you he can't support a wife, and he'll be right."

"His art, he'll—" began Bernice.

"A man of his age who's never made any money isn't going to begin to do it overnight. Stan is quite content with his life as it is. His mother, from what you've told me, not only provides him with a living, but applauds his artistic efforts and supports his ego. When you were safely married to Walter you were quite satisfactory; as a woman in need of a breadwinner, he'll be frightened to death of you. He'll shy off. He'll tell you that you and he were never really suited. He may even get nasty and say you made your bed. He's no good, Bernice."

Bernice's frightened face stared at Victoria, and the telephone rang thinly in the hall.

It was a telegram from Victoria's New York agent. As the operator's mechanical voice spoke, the words fell into capitals on yellow paper: *Schuman has bought "Time to Do" and plans immediate production. Come east as soon as possible. Hallelujah sister you did it at last. John Myron*

The intense elation which welled up in Victoria was strong enough to obliterate completely her friend's trouble from her mind. Her first dream, as a very young writer, had been of a Broadway curtain going up on a scene first imagined in her own mind. That this should have at last begun to happen made her shaky with excitement. She tottered into the dining-room. She placed both hands on the dining-table and leaned her weight on her palms. Then she put one hand to her chest and felt the thump of her heart under the starched white shirt. She straightened, felt a wide smile stretch her mouth. On the wall ahead of her, above the sideboard, was one of the grotesque tin masks from Mexico. The gashed crescent of its mouth was smiling; the slit eyes seemed narrowed with laughter. Victoria threw her arms wide in a gesture which embraced the world. "Now I have everything!" she cried to the mask.

Even as she spoke the words, she became aware of Bernice in the living-room. After a moment of utter silence, "What new everything do you have now?" asked Bernice's tiny voice.

Victoria plunged into the living-room. "My play has sold," she said, trying to make her voice casual.

"Oh," said Bernice. And then, "How wonderful for you, Vicky." The two women looked into each other's faces and found for a moment no other word to say.

Then Bernice began to cry again. Tears ran out of her eyes and down her cheeks. She sat with her still-gloved hands clasped on her lap and cried.

Victoria went to the sofa and put an arm around her shoulders. "Don't!" sobbed Bernice. Victoria drew her arm away. "Not after what you said about Stan."

"You wanted sympathy and I gave you stones," said Victoria. "All right. I'll say what you want to hear. Poor, poor Bernice. Walter is unspeakable. You and Stan will live happily ever after."

"But we won't!" Bernice jerked around so she was facing Victoria. "What you said was true! I've always known it in my heart! Stan is a rotter!" She changed from tears to earnestness. "I'm ruined," she said.

"I don't know why you ever took up with him anyway," Victoria said crossly.

"I was looking for love."

"Oh, God."

"Oh, yes, you can Oh, God. I notice there were quite a few men in your life after you left Sawn."

"That was on my own time," said Victoria. "I wept in my own beer. Don't get shrewish. You've got a problem on your hands. I think I see the way out."

Bernice's face lighted up. She looked almost young again. "Do you, Vicky? Do you?"

"It's this. Walter is taking this stand in order to defend his manhood. But he's very fond of you, and I don't think he really wants to lose you. What he wants is his pride soothed. You can do that. Don't press matters now—he's still too upset."

"Anyway, he's gone to his lodge near Arrowhead," put in Bernice practically.

"Fine. Do nothing, don't try to get in touch with him. Stay

at home; don't move out. When he comes back, tell him that you want his forgiveness, that it's him you want, not Stan."

"And give up Stan?"

"Of course give up Stan!"

"I can't," Bernice wailed. "He's all the love I've ever had!"

Disgust and an old friendship struggled with each other in Victoria. She noted once more that Bernice's chin was starting to sag.

"Love is a luxury you've done without for a good many years," she said brutally. "I'm afraid you're going to keep on doing without it, unless you can find it with Walter. Stan can't support you; you believe you can't support yourself. The best thing for you to do is to forget Stan and try to keep Walter. I sound like the Good Will Hour. But you buttered your bread, Bernice, and now you have to lie in it."

"Everything's so hard, so hard," moaned Bernice. "Nothing ever goes well for me."

"I think you've had a pleasant life," said Victoria.

Suddenly Bernice flared up. Her brown eyes had almost a red color as she spit, "You haven't an ounce of sympathy in you. You're gloating, gloating over what's happened to me. You're glad it's happened!"

The other woman's venom shocked Victoria even while she understood its cause, a rebellion against the hard choice between the penny and the cake. "I'm not glad. I'm sorry, sorry mostly for Walter, but sorry. I'm sorry you ever met Stan. You asked my advice. You don't have to take it. You probably won't. Most people ask advice hoping to be told to do what they want to do. You hoped I'd say everything would be ducky for you and Stan. I won't say it."

Bernice did not reply. She was slumped low on the sofa, staring at the silver tea things before her, her drink tilted forgotten in her black-gloved hand. Victoria straightened it gently. After several minutes of silence, she noticed how dim it was growing in the room, and looked at her watch. A quarter before six. She snapped on the lamp beside the sofa. Bernice started, and looked toward the light, her eyes still blank with thought.

"Listen. Why don't you have dinner here, with Albert and me?"

Bernice shook her head. Victoria saw she had only half heard.

"I ought to change and get things started. Do you want another drink?"

Bernice shook her head again.

Victoria stood up, looked at her friend irresolutely for a moment and then went into the dining-room and down the hall that led to her den and her bedroom beyond. It would do Bernice no harm, she thought, to consider what she had told her.

Victoria had planned to put on a red dress, but decided this would seem too heartless. She chose a short, dressy black one instead, and noticed with pleasure that it made her look quite slender. She brushed her crisp hair, sitting before the mirror of the vanity table beside the high east window, through which cold twilight fell and mingled with the light of the two white lamps. She bent forward and peered at her mirrored reflection.

Her face looked chiseled and durable, as though it had been carved out of a harder substance than Bernice's. She wondered if she had been too unkind; she had wanted so desperately to jog Bernice from her crazy panic, to force her to look at the problem realistically. Bernice usually wept first and thought afterward.

She looked at her wrist watch again. Albert had told her that morning that he would be later than usual tonight; that meant she had a good two hours before she might expect him. The casseroles took fully that long. She snapped off the lights and returned to Bernice.

Bernice's mood had changed. She was in the bright kitchen, washing teacups. Bernice had always been a scrupulous housekeeper. The sugar bowl was back in its proper place on the dining-room sideboard, the silver teapot beside it. Bernice's eyes, slightly reddened from tears, surveyed Victoria's face and then went to her stomach. "Still on your diet?" she asked lightly. "All that weight around your hips is coming back."

The change was almost too much for Victoria. They might have been just discussing anything but catastrophe. "No sugar, no starches," she said.

"That's good." Bernice put the last teacup neatly away in the kitchen cupboard.

"Would you like to stay for supper?" Victoria asked. "Albert won't be home until late."

"Oh, no. I must see Stan. He's meeting me for dinner at six-thirty." Bernice put on her gloves, looked at her watch. "Goodness! I must fly!" The green purse was on the kitchen sideboard. She opened it, surveyed her ravaged face in the mirror of her large flat compact, dabbed powder on her nose. Some of the powder clung to her black glove.

"This is your night for fixing dinner for you and Albert, isn't it?" Bernice asked as she brought out lipstick.

"Yes, my one gesture at domesticity."

Bernice smiled in almost a superior way. "Honestly. How any man *stands* it!" she said.

"Have you decided what you're going to do?" blurted Victoria.

Bernice surveyed her casually around the rim of the open compact. "Oh, yes. I'm going to give up Stan."

Victoria watched her go down the steps to her large, substantial Packard parked in the driveway. Bernice got in, slammed the door after her, waved one black-gloved hand out of the window briefly. As the car drove away Victoria thought how much it looked like a hearse.

Twilight was thickening into night. Victoria had put the casseroles into the oven and was making the coffee. The green coffee canister, one of a row of such canisters on the kitchen sideboard, was nearly empty. A search of the cupboard above revealed no coffee either, and Victoria forgot the problem of her friend Bernice long enough to decide that she would have to scold Hazel in the morning. Hazel was a jewel, but ran to myopia and occasional streaks of absent-mindedness. Her nearsightedness could be forgiven her because she could not help it, but she knew how fond Albert was of his coffee and should not have allowed it to run so low. There was barely enough for three cups. The lower glass globe of the Silex on the stove was just half full. She turned out the gas.

*There,* she thought. *Now there's just the salad to put dressing on, the rolls to heat, and the table to set.* She set the table. She used the pale blue doilies, the gaily painted china. The bowl of bougainvillea from her roof made a fine centerpiece, and she put two white candles at each side of it.

Just as she took the silver sugar bowl from the sideboard and placed it on the table, the doorbell rang. She went to the door expecting Albert, who had been forgetful lately and had probably gone off without his key.

The latch of the top half of the door was stiff, so that it always took a moment to open it. While she was struggling with the latch, the doorbell pealed again. This struck her as odd; Albert knew about the door.

She swung the upper half open, and a gush of cool night air struck her. Light from the room at her back fell brightly on the face looking in at her. Beyond it were the dim round shapes of the hanging ollas of the porch, the dim forms of the trees which hid the house from the street. Something rustled through the ivy that covered the ground below the trees. The crickets had already begun their thin nightly chirping. All this she was conscious of in the flash of time it took her brain to adjust itself to the fact that she was not looking out at the face she had expected to see.

Not Albert. Her first husband, Sawn Harriss, was standing there.

*Chapter Three:*
BAD PENNY

WHENEVER VICTORIA had thought of Sawn during the ten years that followed their divorce, she had thought also of his family, and thinking of them brought two images—the frozen grandeur of crystal chandeliers and the model of a clipper ship under a big bell of glass.

The clipper was one of Grandfather Henry's many ships, all under glass. He collected them. They were his single interest in life besides the managing of the huge family trust fund. Seeing his spare, bright old face peering at her while he explained the rigging of his favorite model, Victoria felt for the first time what she always felt afterward whenever she entered the great old house—the sense of a splendid and forever-vanished past standing just behind her shoulder.

Henry's wife was a handsome old lady who was fond of poetry and travel. Sawn was the only grandchild. Of their two daughters, only Sawn's mother had had a child. She had married a brilliant young engineer upon whose vitality and grasp of life she had come to depend utterly by the time he died in a railroad accident. She had killed herself a year later, when Sawn was six. She was spoken of often by the old people, but in such a euphemistic way that only through Sawn himself had Victoria learned that his mother had taken her own life. Victoria got the feel of a dead woman in whom the old strength had run so thin that one disaster had been too much. Great quiet rooms and Henry's ship models and finishing school had not prepared her for what life had finally given. So her room, remodeled, had become Sawn's. Around the mirror where her cotillion favors had hung, his felt pennants flaunted themselves.

In those early and grim days of the nineteen-thirties, the calm selfishness of these people of Sawn's irritated and amused Victoria. She sat at dinner parties made up of old friends and distant relations, and nothing of the present ever entered there. For all of them it was pleasant times now gone which formed the basis of all conversation, and their talk was like the turning pages of a snapshot album filled with views and faces distant in time. Once, when Victoria introduced the subject of a strike which was filling the newspapers, there was a profound silence. Then Aunt Jessie spoke for them all when she said, reasonably and gently, "These people don't know what real tragedy is. The limited scope of their lives makes them regard such matters as hours and wages as important."

Sawn, however, was of another generation. In college he learned enough to see for the first time the tragic contrasts of the system of which his family was one product and the striking miners another. He went through a period of ruthless bit-

terness which caused his people much suffering, and was once
nearly jailed for hitting a policeman in the eye during a radical
demonstration in New York. By the time Victoria met him he
was a thin young man in full swing of revolt against his people
and what they stood for. He was living in a small dark apartment in lower New York. He had finished his education and
was determined to make his living as a writer. He had sold
three pulp stories, at one cent a word. He was writing a novel
about the scion of a wealthy New England family who revolts
against the environment in which he was born and throws his
lot in with the workers of the world. In Greenwich Village at
that time there were not more than three other young men
writing this same story. His income from the trust fund was
then about five thousand dollars a year.

During their marriage Victoria learned to know him rather
well. His trouble was that he really wanted, intensely wanted,
to spit in the collective eye of his family and tell them what
they could do with their money. But something else in him
prevented this. Some native caution, some fear of his own ability to grapple any more successfully with a hard world than his
mother had grappled. He was in the hands of the past, and half
knew it, even while he desired to escape those clutching fingers and live what he believed. Never admitting this, he tried
to make words substitute for the decisive action which his
youthful mind saw as the proper course. He built up a fence of
words against the uneasy prowling thought that he was living
on the accretions of dead men. Victoria saw no reason why he
should sever his lifeline and throw himself on the mercy of an

economic system not friendly to young writers. All she wanted was for him to face the issue squarely. For his troubling need to escape a sense of guilt often took hazardous and unpleasant means. His undisguised diatribes of contempt against anyone who had a sizable income alienated a number of her friends. Not infrequently he got drunk, coming home late from some revel with the underprivileged. Victoria, working hard editing her small magazine, found such interruptions trying.

But the series of increasingly bitter arguments which reached their climax on the night she left him began over a trifling matter—Sawn's preference for low and noisome bars. Due bills to gay eating-places were one of the perquisites of Victoria's editing job. Sawn scorned such decadent play spots of the economically fortunate, and would insist on going to a hole in the wall infested by cockroaches, cocottes, and cab drivers, where his fondness for liquor was apt to make their evening's bill rather high. Not only did such places depress Victoria, but the financial aspect of the matter annoyed her. She saw in this repeated gesture of Sawn's another futile effort to escape the overly dramatic demands of his own youthful conscience, and she finally taxed him with his elaborate self-deception.

She later decided that was when he began to hate her.

And now he was standing before her. On his shoulders were the two silver bars of a captain. He had grown a mustache, a heavy, dark, aggressively masculine one. His opaque brown eyes showed no emotion. He smiled, and she saw at once that his left upper incisor was a peg tooth, and then wondered how she had noted such a minute change. His face was fuller but still retained the hungry look which had always characterized it. She realized now that it came from the shape of his cheekbones, which were prominent and had shadows below them.

"Hello, little friend," he said in his big, expansive voice. He had always called her that. His use of the old words now conveyed a subtle warning. For some reason of his own he was going to ignore the ten years between them.

She opened the lower half of the door. She realized that although her mind had gone on with the business of making observations, of evoking in one second an entire catalogue of recollections, she was vulnerable to the shock of this re-encounter.

Sawn's shoes made two heavy sounds on the floor. He was smiling as he folded her in a strong embrace and pressed his warm full mouth on hers. His mustache stabbed tiny points of pain into her upper lip. He smelled of whisky. She pushed him away.

He spoke. "You've got quite gray, Victoria!" He sounded surprised, and removed his cap with one tanned hand. His own hair was as dark as ever, and was clipped shorter than he had once worn it. He tossed his cap to the highbacked chair beside the door and let his eyes rove around the room. "This is a nice house," he said. "You've retained your contempt for the flossy things. I wondered if you would."

"I bought this house from a wealthy Mexican who had

managed to make some money out of Mexican oil," she told him.

"How odd," Sawn grinned. "That's the prerogative of the *norteamericanos*. Didn't he know that?"

"I left everything the way it was," went on Victoria, as though it were of great importance that she explain the utterly irrelevant matter of her purchase of the house. Mentally she shook her head. She was not functioning well; Sawn was taking command of the situation.

He looked jauntily around at the dull yellow walls, the bizarre tin masks. "Real adobe," he commented, and added, "I lived three years in Mexico, after I left France in thirty-nine."

"So I understand. Reports of your progress have drifted back to me from time to time."

He looked at her sharply as though seeking for any possible irony under the words. Seeing the strong and self-possessed face before her, she heard a friend's voice which had said, years before, "He's gone very Don Juan. I heard about him from friends in Montmartre. I expected a suave, gigolo sort of person, and got quite a shock when I finally met him. He was insulting a British noblewoman who later became his mistress. He seems to have a peculiar technique. He finds a woman's heel of Achilles and digs at it ruthlessly. Most women seem to like it, at least the rich ones who have been spoiled by their men. Some people think he's a kind of gigolo, but that's not true. It's Dutch treat; he pays his own way and makes the women pay theirs. He gets something out of it besides money.

Maybe just a good roll in the hay. I don't know. But he's a pretty fascinating guy, in his own fashion."

Sawn was rubbing his hands together. Then he reached out and lightly thumped her shoulder. "This is an occasion, old girl. Journey's end. Lovers' meeting. I want a drink."

"You get the ice," said Victoria.

"You're damned tootin' I will. The sight of you coping with an ice tray is one I've never forgotten. Men have conquered nations with less effort."

He filled the Thermos jug on the little bar in the hall with ice cubes. He decided on old-fashioneds to start with. When they were mixed, and as Sawn and Victoria started down to the living-room, Sawn noticed the French door to the right of the dining-table. He went to it and opened it. It led to a small walled balcony. Through trees the lights of Los Angeles could be seen. "I want to sit here," he told her. "I like balconies."

Victoria said dryly, "They have their uses," and went to her bedroom for a short red jacket. When she returned, he had lighted the iron lantern and was stretched out on the long sun chair. Victoria took a deck chair facing it, and as she sank into it realized that she hated deck chairs for the feeling of insecurity they gave her.

"I read your last book," said Sawn. "I can't say I agree with the critics' kind comments."

Victoria sat up straighter. She recalled again what the observant friend had once told her of Sawn. He was starting in on a weak point—her writer's pride.

"You really have no notion of what strange creatures people are, Victoria."

"*Ina Hart* got excellent reviews. The movies bought it."

"Ina would have been a more interesting character if you'd let her curious pattern stand by itself, without so much psychological analysis. She best betrayed her nature by her actions themselves. As we all do. But then psychological analysis was always your favorite pastime. How you used to love to boil a friend down to a shrewd case history!"

"A good many of our friends were case histories. They belonged in a textbook on mildly abnormal psychology."

He grinned. The lantern on the pale wall above him threw down its mild light, reduced his face to hidden eyes, shadows below cheekbones, a black mustache. There was something aggravating about his composure, his sureness.

"How about you?" she demanded. "Did you ever finish the Great American Novel?"

"Who ever does?"

"That trip abroad after the divorce became chronic, didn't it?"

He looked pleased at the nicety of her adjective. "Yes! That's it! Chronic."

"But how about the writing?"

His shoulders drew up in a shrug, and he tossed off the last of his drink. "People and places are more fun than words," he said, and swung easily to his feet. Looking down at her he added, "You need another drink."

"Don't put any sugar in this one. I have to watch my weight."

While he was gone Victoria sat looking at the far lights. There was something sad about them, about the balcony, about the whole situation. Remembrance of things past—mournful words. She recalled for no reason a little song, popular when she had first met Sawn.

> Say it isn't so;
> Say it isn't so.
> Everyone is saying you don't love me.
> Say it isn't so.

On Sunset Strip, below the hill where her house stood, cars were passing in the night. She could not see them because of the balcony wall, but she could hear them. She thought of the long years and what they did to people.

Sawn came back. He handed her a drink. It was cold in her cold hand, in the cold night. "No sugar," he said. Then, standing in front of her and looking down: "It may interest you to know that I've thought of you often, Victoria. I've known a lot of women, some of them beautiful, but you stuck around in my mind."

She could not see his face; his back was to the light. "Is that supposed to throw me into a dither?" she asked.

He sat down on the edge of the long chair, his feet planted wide, his elbows on his knees and the drink in one hand. "In a way, I owe a debt to you. It was your face gone shrewish that night you came home and found the blonde in the shower that told me how little I knew of people. I never expected such a reaction."

"I think it was because she was using my shower cap," said Victoria. "And then, you had on your best pajamas."

He shrugged, and lighted a cigarette. "She meant nothing. I never saw her again. I don't remember her name."

"Yes, you said that night that she meant nothing. You had eaten dinner with some pals on the *Post* and she came over to your table and said she wanted a shower. A tired gal reporter, she was. Wasn't that the story?"

"Something like that."

"But she was really irrelevant. She wasn't the real reason I divorced you."

"No," agreed Sawn. There was something that edged in his voice now. "No, that wasn't the real reason."

"How did you happen to look me up? How did you know I was living in Hollywood?"

"Your name was on the credit titles of a picture I saw when I was stationed near Washington. So when I was shifted out here I looked you up in the phone book. Simple."

He added, "We'll be seeing a lot of each other. Looks as though I'd warm this swivel chair for quite a while."

What happened next occurred swiftly. She turned to set her glass down on the metal table at her elbow. Sawn took the other wrist and drew her smoothly and effortlessly to her feet. He put his arms around her strongly and kissed her hard. He stopped long enough to say, "We were always good together," and then the *kiss* went on.

To be kissed by a man whose kiss she did not desire had for Victoria the element of bathos. The man was at such a disadvantage. But this was different. Sawn was at no disadvantage. His will and his desire were pitted ruthlessly against her. She felt that he was strongly, insolently sure of his ultimate victory.

She ceased struggling, because it seemed only kittenish against his strength. Anger rose and choked her. The fire of the man holding her warmed her cool body, but it fed her anger, not desire.

He released her and stood holding her arms in his strong hands. He held them just below the shoulders and she knew that his fingers would leave bruises. He let her arms go abruptly. She could not see his face; once more the light was behind him. She had the vague notion that if she slapped him he would not be surprised—that he half expected this and knew how to use such a gesture in his own behalf. She said quietly, "Now I'm going to tell you why you did that."

His voice was taunting. "The reason should be fairly obvious to a woman of your experience, little friend."

Her words were each a stone, aimed hard.

"Don Juan the triumphant! So you think. I know what your life has been in these last years. I know why it's been a succession of conquests of women. You Don Juans are all alike. In you is great weakness, which you half suspect. Each woman that you master becomes one more proof that you are strong. You come to believe in yourself, you come to forget the gnawing sense of self-failure that started your abnormal pattern. You strut. But underneath is the rotten core. As you stand there, you're simple to read, with what I already know of you. Once you wanted to cut yourself loose from money you had not earned. You failed to make that gesture out of fear. After I found you out and left you, you had a bad time. You stumbled onto this opiate, and now you're finished. You're an empty

THE BIRTHDAY MURDER · 39

show, put on for yourself. If I didn't understand you I'd despise you."

Sawn made no move, no sound. He was a quiet, faceless bulk standing there with the light behind it.

With a world of anticlimax in the sound, the telephone rang. She turned and left him.

Albert was on the wire. He sounded very tired. "My battery's gone, I think. I've called a garage but I can't get a cab. Could you come after me?"

"Did Leighman sign you up?"

"Not yet."

He described his whereabouts. She hung up the receiver thoughtfully. There was nothing she wanted less than an encounter between Albert and Sawn. Sawn was more than apt to be insufferable, and Albert had had a hard day.

Sawn was stretched out again on the long cushioned chair. He was smoking a cigarette. The tip of it was a red point of fire against his face, now lighted pallidly by the lantern above his head. He turned his eyes sideways and looked up at her. His posture and the slow movement of his eyes made her think of a sick man.

Buttoning the top of her scarlet jacket she said, "I'm going to pick up my husband. Can I drop you off somewhere?"

Slowly he sat up, staring at her left hand. "I didn't see your wedding ring." He added, "You were listed as Victoria Jason."

"Yes, I've only been married six months."

Sawn stood up. "Who is he?"

"His name's Albert Hime."

"Albert Hime," repeated Sawn, and walked toward the balcony wall.

"I've got to leave. Get your cap."

He shook his head, looking at the twinkling lights. "I think I should meet your husband. Yes. I've decided that I want to meet your husband." He took a deep puff of his cigarette.

"But I don't want you to."

"That's too bad."

His voice was flat and a little nasty. She knew that the more she might argue, the more obdurate he would become. "Suit yourself then. It really makes no difference to me." She made her own voice as emotionless as his had been.

Moodily he flipped the cigarette over the balcony wall, watched it arc down into darkness. She got the feel of a great irresolution in him, and of a weariness. As she left him standing there she knew that the elaborate structure which had sustained his ego for many years was lying in ruins at his feet.

## Chapter Four:
## DEATH BEFORE BREAKFAST

As THEY drove back home in her open car with the wind of their passage whipping their faces, Victoria told Albert of Sawn's return. He showed only mild interest.

"It's the damnedest thing," she said, "to see a face that was your sun and sky ten years ago and feel nothing of the old emotion."

"I know what you mean," Albert said. "I saw Della a few years ago. To get to something relevant, Moira says you don't think much of her as Ina."

"I don't."

"Leighman seems rather taken with her. He and I dropped past her apartment tonight after we left the studio. She and her agent were just leaving for dinner. We had coffee with them, and I thought Leighman seemed rather taken."

"He won't be after I talk with him."

"Are you sure you can handle Leighman?"

"I'm certain of it."

Albert sighed. "I wish I knew definitely," he said irritably, "about producing *Ina.*"

"George always wavers like mad before making any important decision. Anyway, he's not the final word. There's the vice-president over him."

"It seems that the studio's leaving the matter of the producer entirely up to Leighman." He added grumpily, "Why don't we eat out tonight? I don't want to meet any ex-husbands the way I feel right now."

"The casseroles are in the oven," said Victoria. She added, thinking of Sawn, "All right. I'll take them out and we'll go down to Chasen's."

"You're a darling."

"Correct me if I'm wrong. It seems to me that you've got pretty interested in the career of this Hastings gal. I'm nothing if not broad-minded, but I like to know where things stand."

"Remember what I said once about pretty little things?" Albert asked. "I haven't changed my mind."

The first thing Victoria saw when they entered the house was that Sawn's cap was gone from the chair by the door. She went swiftly to the balcony. The light shone down on empty chairs. She called Sawn's name. There was no answer. Albert was standing beside the dining-table rubbing his temples and watching her. "You have the queerest look on your face."

"He's gone," she said. "So we don't have to go to Chasen's after all."

"All right," said Albert.

She went to the kitchen, and at once saw the cup and saucer

on the drainboard by the sink. A little coffee was pooled in the bottom, "Damn," she said, aloud. That left only two cups in the Silex. She decided not to mention this to Albert. He might feel that it provided a good reason to go to Chasen's after all. She thought of the sleek café, the waiting for a table, the wait for food. *We can go tomorrow night,* she thought, *to celebrate my birthday.*

Before they sat down to dinner, Albert kissed her.

While they ate she told him about her play. He seemed delighted. They had finished their casseroles and she had poured their coffee from the silver pot when the telephone rang. "I'll get it," she said.

Bernice's small, tear-stained voice said, "Vicky?"

"Yes, darling."

"Stan made a dreadful fuss, but he never once suggested that I should leave Walter and marry him."

"I thought he wouldn't."

"Have you eaten dinner?"

"Yes."

"Oh. Well, I just wanted to tell you how things went."

"Are you with him now?"

"He's waiting for me at our table."

"If you were really smart you'd leave him waiting."

"Oh, I couldn't do that."

"Remember that it has to be a clean break."

Bernice's voice was almost passionate. "Is any break clean? Haven't you ever heard the saying, 'To say good-by is to die a little?'" She added, rather unnecessarily, Victoria thought, and with considerable dislike in her tone, "But then I suppose it was never like that for you. You feel with your head instead of your heart."

"You think with your emotions."

"If it doesn't work out the way you think it will, I've lost out every way," moaned Bernice.

"You haven't lost much in Stan."

Bernice slammed down the receiver.

When Victoria returned to the table, Albert was looking down into his empty coffee cup. He was frowning.

"That was Bernice. Walter's found out about Stan."

He looked up, interested. "Oh?"

"He wants a divorce. I can't say I blame him."

"No, you can't blame him."

The telephone rang again. "That thing hasn't been still for five minutes at a stretch all day," Victoria commented. "I'm thinking of having it jerked out and relying entirely on carrier pigeons."

Albert smiled slightly as he stood up. "My turn."

While his voice murmured in the hall, Victoria thought about the events of the afternoon. It had certainly been a full one. She took one sip of her coffee. It was only lukewarm. She carried it to the kitchen and heated it in the Silex. She thought of Sawn, walking about her house, completely at home; pouring coffee for himself, drinking it in her kitchen. It was typical of him. She wondered what had made him decide to leave. She returned to the dining-room. Thinking of Sawn, she felt rich in having Albert. She looked down at her hand tilting the glass globe of the Silex above her empty cup. She went to Albert's place and gave the coffee to him. Returning to the kitchen, she set the empty Silex on the stove and then from the kitchen doorway she saw Albert return to his place at the end of the table. He was in profile to her, and his face seen that way looked closed to her and abstracted. For the first time she felt that perhaps she had not entered enough into Albert's problems. He laid his napkin across his knees. He put two spoonfuls of sugar in his coffee and stirred it thoughtfully.

"Who was it?" Victoria asked as she went to her place at the long table's opposite end.

"Moira Hastings. It seems I left my script in the café where we all talked. She wanted to tell me it was all right. She has it."

"Did she say any more about the part?"

"At length."

"What did you tell her?"

He looked up in some surprise. "I told her no, of course."

"Well," she asked, "was it such a bad dinner?"

"It was very good. You're turning into quite a cook."

Victoria said modestly, "Oh, it wasn't anything to fix."

"I wonder what made Harriss run out."

"Maybe he'd had enough drama for one evening. I had to tell him what I thought of him."

"Oh?"

"He's turned into something not too nice. He's one of those hollow men who get physical virility and real manhood confused with one another. I told him so. I left him with a lot to think about. It's too late, of course."

Albert's response surprised her. "Sometimes," he said, "I find you a little hard, Victoria."

They rinsed all the dinner dishes, a Thursday-night custom since the summer influx of ants. They went to bed at eleven, in their separate rooms. Sleep did not come at once to Victoria. There was a party going on in the big house next door. The house was a little higher than hers because of the upward slope of the hill, and looking out the window at the foot of her bed she could see the lighted windows staring down at her through the trees of the narrow side yard. She closed the curtains and lay there in the darkness. Someone began to play the piano in the house next door. Someone who played quite well, but with the touch of a dilettante. Like Sawn. It sounded like Sawn playing in the apartment they had shared so many years ago. The pianist played *Happy Birthday to You.*

She took a sleeping pill. As she settled back against the pillow, she heard from the hall the faint sound of dialing. She wondered who Albert could be telephoning at such a late hour. Propping herself up on one elbow she listened. Albert was speaking very softly, but she heard him ask the operator for Western Union. A burst of merriment from the house next door obscured what he said next. When the laughter had died down somewhat, she could hear him speaking in the slow, pausing voice of one dictating a telegram. ". . . appreciate all speed possible. Birthday gift. Send to Mrs. Hime, above address." She dropped back against her pillow, smiling. Albert had forgotten her birthday; that song next door had reminded him of it. She wondered what gift he had ordered for her.

Sleep closed in snugly about her. The pianist next door was playing again, a medley of old songs which had been popular in the year she and Sawn had lived together. *Stardust, La-*

*zybones,* and one which she didn't think anyone remembered now, *Farewell to Arms.* She found herself swallowed up by the eerie feeling of sliding back, back in time. The pianist played *Stormy Weather.* Faintly she heard a woman's voice take up the words, ". . . since my man and I ain't together, keeps rainin' all the time, keeps rainin' all the ti—me."

So long ago, now—

She dreamed that night of an apartment overlooking the flat breadth of the Hudson River, the palisades of New Jersey stretched along the opposite shore. Sawn sitting at the spinet piano, playing and smiling as he played. A blond woman with the face of Bernice and with eyes swimming with tears leaned against the piano and said, "To say good-by is to die a little." And Sawn kept on smiling and playing and the blonde went away. He stopped playing then and stood up from the piano and came toward Victoria across the soundless thick rug, and she was wildly afraid and called for Albert, but he was making a telephone call.

She awoke at seven. After she had showered she put on a housecoat on which yellow daffodils romped over a gray-blue background. She recalled dismally that there was no coffee in the house. She would have to drink milk. Or cocoa. She wondered about borrowing some coffee from Humphrey Bogart's cook. But she didn't want to cross the street in a housecoat. She decided to drink milk.

She knew Albert would want to reach the studio early. He would have to eat breakfast at the commissary. She went down the hall that led to his room to wake him.

The door was shut. She opened it and it stopped with a

bump against something hard. She squeezed through the half-open door to see what had stopped it from opening. She looked down and saw that it was Albert's head.

He was lying in a curious, crouched position on the floor near the door. His elbows were close to his body, his hands were under his stomach. He had on blue pajamas with a maroon stripe. His mouth was open, the side of his head was pressed against the floor. Before she screamed she knew she would never wake Albert. Albert was dead.

*Chapter Five:*
## THE MILLS OF THE COPS

DR. MAHLER straightened slowly and stood looking down at Albert's body. Victoria watched him from the doorway, holding the edge of the door frame for support. Dr. Mahler rubbed his wide hands together with a dry, sliding sound. The room was very still.

Dr. Mahler turned toward Victoria. His broad face, a little like a personable Eskimo's, was startlingly grave without the wide smile it usually wore. "He's been poisoned," he said quietly. "I'll have to telephone the police, Victoria."

She heard her own voice, shrill and strained. "I don't understand this. I don't understand it at all. And I think I'm going to fall over."

He came toward her. His voice was soothing. "I'll give you a sedative, and then you'd better lie down for a while." His hand took her forearm, impersonally gentle. He turned her around, led her down the hall outside Albert's room. They passed the bathroom and turned into Victoria's den, beyond which her big bedroom lay, disheveled from the night.

"No," said Victoria, stopping in her tracks, "I don't want to go to bed."

His voice was still soothing. "Best place in the world to get over a shock."

"No! The police will want to question me. I don't want to be questioned in bed."

With no word, he turned and walked her down the hall that led to the dining-room. "Please don't hang onto me," she snapped. "I'll be all right."

After a moment's hesitation, his hand left her arm. She went into the dining-room and marched stiffly past the long table now bare and gleaming in the morning light. The cerise bougainvillea that had graced the dinner table the night before were now wilted in their white bowl. She heard the swift sound of dialing, and then Dr. Mahler's low voice, speaking in the hall behind her. She could not seem to concentrate on his words.

She lay down on the sofa in the living-room, closing her eyes against the muffled glare that beat against the orange curtains of the big window behind it. Her foot touched something and she saw it was the script of the movie adaptation of *Ina Hart*, still lying as she had left it the day before. She made an impatient movement with her foot and the manuscript struck the big brown tiles of the floor with a muffled thud.

She heard footsteps coming toward her and opened her eyes. Dr. Mahler was passing the dining-room table. A glass of water was in one hand. He sat down on the edge of the sofa and held it out to her. On the broad palm of the other hand was a small white capsule. The pores of his unfamiliarly grave face were very large, as though down the years his usually ebullient spirits had slowly expanded the skin. Victoria propped herself up on one elbow, obediently took the pill from his one hand, the glass of water from the other. The excessive dryness of her throat, which she had not noticed before, made her choke a little. Dr. Mahler patted her three times on the back and took the glass from her. She lay down nervelessly and closed her eyes.

"When you wake up, the police will probably be here. I've telephoned them. I am going to call your servant, and I think I'll call Mrs. Saxe, too, and have her rally around."

"Oh, Lord, not Bernice," said Victoria, impatiently. "She's got her own troubles."

"But no trouble to compare with this," said Dr. Mahler.

"Was it food poisoning?" Victoria asked. "Botulism? The stuff you get from eating toadstools?"

Dr. Mahler hesitated, and she opened her eyes just as his mouth moved in answer. "I don't know what poison."

Victoria closed her eyes again. There was a silence, and it seemed to her that Dr. Mahler's eyes were going over her face carefully and coolly. Then he moved abruptly, the divan stirring under her in response to his action. She opened her eyes and saw that his thick body was bending forward. He picked something up from the floor. It was the script of *Ina Hart*. He sat holding it in one hand, looking down at it curiously. Then he put it on the coffee table and stood up. His eyes were still on it as he rose.

When he saw Victoria watching him, he jerked his head toward the manuscript. "Funny," he said.

"Yes. It's funny," she echoed.

. She knew what he was thinking. That Ina Hart had poisoned her husband. She knew he was remembering the afternoon a year before when she had sat in his office, poring over a thick book about poisons—their availability, their deadliness.

He looked at his wrist watch with a stiff motion that seemed forced. "I have to go. I have a call to make at nine-thirty." He looked at her with professional concern. "Don't fight it. When you get drowsy, let yourself drop off to sleep. You'll feel a lot better, a lot clearer when you wake up."

"All right," said Victoria.

"What's Hazel's phone number?"

"It's in the green book by the phone."

"Is Mrs. Saxe's there too?"

"Yes."

Watching his broad dark back go plodding down the narrow dining-room, Victoria suddenly wondered if he had gone to the kitchen for the glass of water with which she had taken the pill. And if he had, whether he had seen that one of the row of green canisters near the sink had on its side a red-edged label on which Hazel had printed in large capitals the words *Ant Poison.*

It was with ant poison that Ina Hart had killed her husband.

Victoria lay wide-awake, doubting that the sedative he had given her would work. While she lay there she looked about the room. On the wall opposite the sofa the three tin masks stared down. Their smooth convex surfaces held light coldly in the dimmed room. The central one had a feather headdress, feathers made of tin. The other two were smaller and had less ornate headdresses. The mouths were crescent-shaped; two turned up, one turned down. All the eyes were narrow, slanted and pointed at either end. Through the slits that were the eyes the blank wall showed.

Dr. Mahler returned from the telephone and sat heavily in the chair below the masks.

"You needn't wait; I'll be all right."

"I'll wait until Hazel comes," he said.

The last thing she saw before stupor took her was his broad, sober face, watching her.

Richard Tuck, of the Los Angeles Homicide Squad, was regarded by his colleagues as being a rather queer duck. Concerning his own understanding of crime, he possessed a humility against which their glib cynicism rang hollow and empty. He seemed careless of achieving a record for speedily winding up cases in which he was involved, and showed instead a disinclination to make an arrest without substantial evidence. The result of this odd quirk was that no case of his which had come to trial had ever been lost by the state. This gave him a definite standing with Gufferty, the head of the Homicide Squad, and, which was more important, with the District Attorney's office. A number of detectives were jealous of him. And yet his convincing unconcern robbed their jealousy of much point, and left many of them with a sense of most annoying frustration regarding all six feet five inches of Richard Tuck.

They could never understand why when violent death left its usual haunts on the wrong side of the tracks and entered a home in Beverly Hills, a Los Angeles university or other such genteel places, it was Tuck whom Gufferty placed in charge, rather than one of themselves. It certainly wasn't that he was a smooth man; he was a slow man, and his inevitable brown suit was apt to want pressing. He took down his own notes in a strange private shorthand. He was grudging in giving information to reporters, yet somehow managed to retain their liking. They called him "The Moose." His final report of a case was long, involved, painstaking, watertight, and written in a flawless, if rather pedestrian, English prose.

Of his private life it was known that he lived alone in a house on a hill in the northeastern part of town, that he sometimes went to concerts, that he had no visible family and few friends. Apparently his work and his mild pleasures were all he wanted. It was also known that he had once been married to a woman named Lucy, and that it was his sudden decision to join the police force as a common, blue-uniformed, foot-slogging policeman which had directly caused the divorce in which the brief marriage had terminated.

E. Byron Froody usually worked with Tuck. Froody was a little fat man with sad green eyes, a waddling walk which had gamed him the epithet "Duck Butt"(of which he always pretended to be unaware), and an admiration of Tuck which would have been embarrassing to many men. Froody loved all niggling detail; he was the perfect leg man. He never swore; he knew his Sherlock Holmes by heart, and his Tarzan almost as well. He clipped poetry from the editorial page of the city's most conservative newspaper and kept it for weeks in his wallet. His private life was as colorless as Tuck's own.

So these two went their ways apart from the others and did not seem to mind. They gradually gained a certain distinction. The other members of the squad at last adopted toward them the contemptuously affectionate attitude.

A large, pretty woman opened the door of the little Mexican house to Tuck and Froody. In spite of the dark circles below her brown eyes she had about her that flush of subdued excitement which grips certain women at a time of sudden tragedy in which they themselves are not personally involved. She had on a suit of soft blue wool, and the color seemed to Tuck too young for her ripe body, her large face. She said in a whisper, "Shh. She's asleep."

She stood aside to let them enter and Tuck could see the form of a woman, covered by a blanket, lying on the sofa in the living-room. He could see only a fluff of gray hair, a sharp, closed face. She was lying on her back. "Is that Mrs. Hime?" he asked.

The large pretty woman nodded. "I'm Bernice Saxe," she said in a small voice. "Dr. Mahler called me after he phoned you. I'm Victoria's oldest friend, you see."

Tuck heard a subdued sound in the kitchen. "That's Hazel, Mrs. Hime's maid," said Bernice Saxe. "She's been with her for three years, and can tell you anything you want to know."

"First I want to see Mr. Hime," said Tuck.

Bernice Saxe pointed down the narrow dark hall leading off to the left. "He's in there, I think."

"You haven't seen the body?"

Bernice Saxe's shoulders drew up in something like a shudder. "I've been in the kitchen talking to Hazel."

Tuck noted at once the curious posture of the dead man, Albert Hime. The two big policemen who had been talking quietly when he entered the bedroom snapped to something like attention, gave him their meager information. The dead man was a film producer. He had died from some sort of poison. His wife had not discovered it until the morning because they had separate rooms. "There's an inkstain on his right forefinger," added the smaller policeman, and Tuck duly noted that there was. He excused them.

They had no sooner gone than the medical examiner arrived, accompanied by a photographer, a fingerprint expert and two young reporters. Tuck stopped the reporters at the door and gave them the basic facts. As they had barely time to make the next edition they left docilely. When he re-entered Albert Hime's bedroom, the medical examiner was completing his cursory first survey. "Can't tell much until after the p.m., except that the doctor who reported the case was right. This man has been poisoned. He's been dead for approximately ten hours. Say since between one and three in the morning. It wasn't one of the caustic poisons; I don't think it was a narcotic, either, but I'm not sure yet."

"From the position of the body," Tuck said, "it looks as

though the last painful symptoms had set in fast. It looks as though he started to feel bad, maybe woke up with a belly pain, lay wondering whether he had indigestion, got up and started to the door to get some soda or a doctor and keeled over onto the floor."

"It does look that way," agreed the medical examiner. "Didn't he have a wife? Where was she?"

"Separate bedrooms," said Tuck.

"Humph," said the medical examiner. "Most poisons have acutely painful final symptoms, preceding coma. She must be a hard sleeper."

"She seems to be," said Tuck mildly, thinking of the woman on the sofa. He turned and looked down at Froody beside him. "Take a good look around for some poison," he said. Froody nodded and bustled out.

After a scrupulous examination of the room, which offered nothing, Tuck left the photographer, the fingerprint man and the medical examiner at work and returned to the kitchen. The servant, a tiny woman with white hair, a pink sweater and a blurred expression due to her excessively thick rimless eyeglasses, was pouring sudsy water out of an enamel dishpan. Mrs. Saxe, smoking a cork-tipped cigarette, watched in a desultory way. Tuck pointed a long finger at the dishwater. "What have you been washing?" he asked sternly.

"The dinner dishes," replied the servant. Her voice was soft and blurred too, and behind their glasses her pallid eyes flashed onto his face and then were gone.

"Don't you know enough not to touch any possible evidence

when a man has died of poison, may have been murdered?" asked Tuck.

"Murdered!" said Bernice Saxe sharply. The long ash tumbled unheeded from the tip of her cigarette.

"I'm not a detective," said the servant with meek tartness. "I always do the dishes when I come in mornings. And anyhow they were all rinsed. Mr. and Mrs. Hime always rinse them."

Tuck turned to Bernice Saxe. "Certainly the idea of murder must have occurred to you, Mrs. Saxe."

"It's too fantastic," said Bernice Saxe, but did not say why.

"My name's Tuck," Tuck told them, mechanically showing his badge. He turned to the servant. "What's your name?"

"Hazel Bennett. Mrs. Hazel Bennett."

"Mrs. Saxe says you've worked for Mrs. Hime for three years. Do you know any reason why Mr. Hime could have taken his own life?"

Hazel shook her head rather dully. It was Bernice Saxe who elaborated. With the ash long again on her cigarette which she held, Tuck noted, at an affected tilt in her hand, she spoke from the kitchen stool on which she was rather gracefully ensconced. "I've known him only six months or so, from the time they were married, but I'd say no. I mean, to commit suicide a person has to have—well, a sort of passionate quality. Albert was—well, he was *quiet*. He was a matter-of-fact person. I can't imagine him killing himself over anything."

"That seems to leave accident or murder, then," said Tuck, and watched them.

Mrs. Saxe slipped from the stool, her high heels clattering on the floor, "It can't be murder!" she exclaimed, with what seemed to Tuck undue passion. "It just can't be." She added, staring into his eyes with her shining brown ones, "I mean, they were such a devoted couple."

Hazel's little gray head turned toward Mrs. Saxe and at the same moment the friend of Mrs. Hime seemed to realize the implication of what she had said, and abruptly lowered her lids over her eyes.

As Tuck turned to leave the kitchen he told them, "You'd better wake Mrs. Hime now. I have to talk to her. You might give her some black coffee."

"There isn't any coffee," said Hazel. "I was just going to the store to get some."

"Go right ahead," said Tuck.

In the narrow hall leading back to the bedrooms Tuck came face to face with Froody. Froody, a white handkerchief around his hand, was holding out a cardboard box about six inches high. "Look!" he said.

Tuck moved so that light from the window above the recessed bar fell on the yellow box. It had a fine coating of dust and bore the legend *Fuller's Ant Poison*. It had been opened.

"I found it on the top shelf of the cupboard in the den," said Froody. "It was shoved way back."

The medical examiner turned into the hall from the dead man's room, his bag in his hand, his hat on his head. Tuck held out the box which he had taken from Froody in order to read the fine print containing a list of the ingredients of Fuller's ant powder. "Ninety percent sodium fluoride," Tuck said to the medical examiner. "Would you say a dose of this could have killed Hime?"

"Sodium fluoride," repeated the doctor. He cocked his head to one side. "Yes. That could have done the trick. I'd say that—oh, about a teaspoonful would kill—" he let his eyes rove up Tuck's height—"even you."

"I think I'll take a look at this den," said Tuck. He used two sheets from the stack of yellow paper on the desk to wrap the box of poison carefully.

"Someone around here must be a writer," said Froody, nodding toward the typewriter, the deep stack of pages beside it.

"Mrs. Hime," said Tuck, looking at the first page of the manuscript. "She calls herself Victoria Jason."

Before Victoria awoke, she dreamed.

*New York City. 1924. Public School 132. A Field Day in Van Cortlandt Park. The sloping wooden bleachers overlooking the oval field. The white middy blouses and red silk ties of the little girls blaring in the sun, fluttering in the sun of the bleachers. The hoarse-voiced little boys. Beyond the bleachers the silver mirror of the little lake. The spectacular sound of the blank cartridge fired by the boys' gym instructor at the start of each race.*

*Thin little Victoria in her element. Poor Bernice could only run in the girls' relay races, blundering along behind the others, handing the stick of wood to Victoria, who sprang forward, caught up with the others, imagining herself a Greek runner, a woman Greek runner, carrying a message which would save Johnny Vente's life.*

*The boys' gym instructor blowing the bright whistle hanging around his neck, announcing the eighth and ninth-grade girls' fifty-yard dash. Except for the eighth and ninth-grade boys' dash, this was the most important race of the day. To the home room of the*

*winner would pass the custody for the rest of the term of a large-sil-
ver cup with a slight dent near one handle.*

*Victoria trotting to the starting line, the pit of her stomach emp-
ty with excitement. Forcing herself not to look toward the bleachers,
not to try to single out Johnny Vente's face. "On mark!" The toe of
her canvas sneaker edging out into the white powder of the starting
line. "Set!" Her finger tips down on the soft warm dust. "Go!" The
agonizing forward lunge and then the legs running, running. A
woman Greek runner, bearing a message that would save Johnny
Vente's life.*

*Over so soon. The sudden horizontal tape ahead. The arms flung
upward, the tape breasted and broken. The shrill roar from the children on the bleachers. Victoria. Victoria.*

*And Victoria, small, hot, and panting, pulling up the leg of one
black sateen bloomer, casting bright glances among the boys and
girls who swarmed around the finish line. No Johnny. No Bernice.*

*The pink moist face of Adele. Her giggle. Her whisper, behind
one hand. "Lissen. It's awful. They rented a rowboat. They're row-
ing on the lake. Bernice and Johnny Vente. When Miss Jacobs finds
out—!"*

*The little lake, a silver mirror in the sun. Miss Jacobs stalking to
the dock at its margin, followed by an excited, whispering horde of
boys and girls. The loving cup bright and cool in Victoria's arms. The
trumpet of Miss Jacobs's wrath as she stood on the dock, calling the
sinners in. Bernice, stepping out of the rowboat under Miss Jacobs's
hard black eyes. Bernice's eyes looking for Victoria, finding her. The
strange look of triumph on Bernice's plump pretty face, even while
Miss Jacobs's tongue lashed her. Bernice, glamorous in her known,
red-handed sinning. Bernice's day. Not Victoria's.*

A hand closed on Victoria's shoulder. First the hand belonged to someone in that June of 1924, and then Victoria opened her eyes and saw Bernice, in pale blue, bending over her. They looked into each other's eyes.

"You know what I was just remembering?" Victoria asked her, dreamily. "I was remembering that Field Day when you went boating with Johnny Vente."

Bernice's shiny brown eyes, which had been empty of anything but watching, clouded over with recollection. Her tiny voice said, "Yes. I remember."

And then Victoria saw the three tin masks on the wall beyond Bernice, and it was now, and Albert was dead.

"Oh, my God!" she whispered. For the first time the enormous truth dawned on her. Albert was really dead. Their short time together was at an end. She felt tears start into her eyes. "Albert's dead," she told Bernice. "Somehow, Albert's dead."

"Shhh!" soothed Bernice. "I know all about it. Everything's all right, Victoria. His secretary phoned to find why he hadn't come to the studio. I just told her he wouldn't be out and to call you tomorrow."

Victoria shook her head dazedly. Then a new thought struck her. "The police!"

"Shhh. They're in there where Albert is."

For the first time Victoria became aware of footsteps in the house. A giant in a brown suit entered the dining-room. He came toward them. Victoria was not wearing her harlequin glasses; she saw him in detail only as he reached the three shallow steps leading down into the living-room. His hair was the color of a wet seal. His long face, both tan and sallow, had deep grooves at either side of the firm, full-lipped mouth. His eyes were narrow, of a clear brown, and they looked as though they would never be surprised at anything.

When he was standing beside Bernice, making the large woman seem diminutive, he looked down at Victoria and said, "I'm Lieutenant Tuck, of the Los Angeles Homicide Squad." Lieutenant Tuck's voice seemed to have adjusted itself to a world of people who were smaller than he. It was a voice held under control.

Tuck turned then to Bernice. "I prefer to have no one else present when I'm questioning a witness."

Bernice's voice, coming after his, seemed thin and a little frightened. "Oh. Oh, of course." She turned to Victoria and said, stiltedly, "I'll come by later, darling."

Then he seated himself in a chair facing the sofa. The chair was too small for him. His eyes had a dogged, patient look, as though he were used to being cramped in chairs that were too small for him. He drew a black notebook from an inner coat pocket, found a yellow pencil in another pocket. Victoria was suddenly aware that a housecoat on which daffodils romped was unhappily inappropriate attire for a woman whose husband has just died. She was also aware that her hair badly needed combing. As she struggled to a sitting position, she saw on the coffee table between them the script of *Ina Hart*.

"Do you know of any reason why your husband might have taken his life?" asked Lieutenant Tuck.

Victoria gathered herself together. "No. He was not an emotional man. And he was too much of an egoist to take his life in any circumstances."

Mr. Tuck's forehead wrinkled into horizontal creases as he raised his eyebrows.

"Look," said Victoria. "I realize that there are certain conventional poses to be adopted by a bereaved wife. You want the truth. I'm a writer, and people are my business, and I probably know more about Albert than anyone alive. And his death does not canonize him."

Tuck said, "We're going to get on well, Mrs. Hime."

They did. Mr. Tuck asked innumerable questions; Victoria answered with all the precision she could muster. Their quiet voices in that quiet room came to have a fantastic sound to her, as though the two of them were playing an elaborate word game while outside the orange-curtained windows the world lay in the ruins of some final Armageddon.

Although the long face opposite her remained impassive during most of the questioning, the impassivity broke three times. The first time was when he said, "I have been wondering why you did not hear some disturbance in the night. Although the symptoms preceding coma and death must have been brief, they must also have been very painful. He certainly would have called for you. Yet you did not hear him."

"I had taken a sleeping pill."

Then came the reaction. Mr. Tuck's brows rose and the forehead folded into creases.

"I often do," Victoria said defensively. "And last night the people next door were having a loud party."

"It's an excellent explanation of why you didn't hear him," he said mildly. Victoria had the notion that it might seem a little too excellent.

The second reaction came when she said she had in part prepared and had served the last meal Albert ate, and that just the two of them had dined together. She explained about the Thursday night casserole. Once more Mr. Tuck's forehead creased.

"You also ate some of this casserole?"

"Yes."

There was a moment's silence while Tuck jotted down these facts. It was some dozen questions later that he asked, "Didn't it occur to you to leave word to your servant not to wash those supper dishes? You knew from what Dr. Mahler had told you that your husband had been poisoned. Didn't it occur to you that he might have died from something he ate in this house, and that the soiled dishes constituted possibly important evidence?"

"No," said Victoria. "It didn't occur to me that he could have died from something he ate here. Because he couldn't have. We both ate exactly the same food. From the same casserole, the same salad bowl, the same pot of coffee. Wait. I didn't have any coffee; there wasn't enough for both of us. And, yes, Albert used some sugar. I didn't."

"Do you know whether your husband had anything to eat or drink before he came home?"

"Yes. He happened to mention that he had a cup of coffee with some business associates."

She gave him the names of Moira Hastings, George Leighman and Louis Lester. "You see," she said, "Albert was going to produce a picture called *Ina Hart*. Leighman was the executive producer who was about to give him the as-

signment. Miss Hastings was being considered for the part—
she's too inexperienced to play it, though—and Louis Lester
was her agent."

It was then that Tuck's eyes fell on the script of *Ina Hart* on
the table between them. Below the title were the words, *From
the novel by Victoria Jason*. "I'm Victoria Jason," she told him.
She added, and heard the note of defiance in her own voice,
"It's the story of a woman who poisons her husband."

That was when Tuck's brow clouded for the third time.

Two things happened then. Hazel pattered out of the
kitchen, down the dining-room, carrying a tray containing two
steaming cups of black coffee. As she put it down on the table
between them, the doorbell rang. Tuck stood up. "That's probably the coroner's ambulance," he said. He added, "You'll want
to go to your room. I believe we're through in there."

The desire to refuse the offered kindness was strong in Victoria. She wanted to say, "I don't mind seeing Albert go," but
she said, "Thank you," in an unnatural voice, and stood up also,
drawing the gay housecoat about her.

At the top of the steps to the dining-room Mr. Tuck
turned long enough to say gravely, "I don't believe I care for
any coffee."

Victoria stood in the center of the red and gray Navaho
rug on the floor of her den. Her hands were clenched at her
sides. Outside the closed brown door she heard footsteps coming from the direction of Albert's room. Careful, sliding footsteps, those of men carrying a weight between them. The queer
thought struck her that now there were only the expensive
suits hanging limp from their polished hangers in the closet

of the guest room, and the big English clothesbrush on the highboy.

She turned sharply and sat down on the hard chair before her desk as though an alteration of her position could alter her thoughts. An emotion was gathering in the core of her body, an emotion to which she could not at first attach a name. Then she realized what it was. Fear. She was afraid, afraid of what she could not understand. There was no reason, no sense to Albert's dying.

Someone tapped at her door. "All right," she said. "You can come in."

It was Lieutenant Tuck. She stood up, her desk between them. The fact that he paid no attention to the room told her that he had already seen it. The thought of his big hands going through the papers on her desk brought with it a muffled sense of violation. "I'm going to ask you not to leave here for the present," he said. "After I get the results of the autopsy I'll want to talk to you again. This has been groping in the dark, because we had so little to go on."

"I had no intention of going away," she replied stiffly, still unreasonably resentful of the fact that he had undoubtedly entered her sanctum while she lay sleeping.

"I'll be back as soon as possible," he said. "It all depends on how quickly the coroner comes to his conclusions. That depends on when the poison which killed your husband was taken. If it is still in the stomach the autopsy will take no time at all. On the other hand, if it was a slow poison, taken some time ago, and the kidneys and intestines are involved, it may take days for the analysis of these organs. I'm explaining this so that you will understand that you must be patient for the truth about your husband's death."

"I understand," said Victoria.

"I'd like the addresses of those people your husband had the coffee with."

"George Leighman is in the little green book next to the phone. Louis Lester is in the phone book, and you can get Miss Hastings's address from him."

"Thank you."

After he had gone, Victoria went to her bedroom and looked through the clothes in her closet for a black dress. There was one formal dinner gown, and the dress she had worn the night before. She was stepping into the leg of her navy-blue slack suit when Hazel came in. "I borrowed that coffee from the Bogarts' cook," she said. "I was wondering if I should go down to the store now, or if you'd rather have me stay here with you."

"Go on to the store," Victoria told her. She thought of how she had intended the night before to scold Hazel mildly about the dearth of coffee. It seemed very irrelevant now.

Hazel hovered. Victoria looked up at her from the red play shoe she was putting on. "What is it, Hazel?"

Hazel's face was soft with pity. "Don't you worry, dear," she said. "It's as plain as a pipestem. Mr. Hime got something that poisoned him in one of those restaurants he liked so much. Just because they're fancy in front doesn't mean a clean kitchen."

"Roaches in the Waldorf?" asked Victoria.

"Why, only last winter there were all those people poisoned

with crab meat. I forget the name of the place, but it was one of these fancy Hollywood ones," Hazel said. "That's what happened. That's the only way it could have been. When they get through that autopsy or whatever they call it, they'll find I'm right. I told Mr. Tuck that before he left."

"What did he say?"

"He said it was quite possible," Hazel replied.

This soothed Victoria, and stilled the chaos of her thoughts. "Yes," she said. "That's the only way it could have been, after all."

When Hazel had gone, Victoria thought for the first time of another alternative. She recalled that a month before, Hazel had filled the sugar bowl with salt. She had reached for the wrong green canister.

It was impossible that she should find herself taking place in a tragic farce. It was impossible that she should become for all the world the enigmatic creature called into being by the fleeting notion that Albert had died from a dose of ant poison. It was impossible that she should become the Victoria Jason Hime whose husband had died of ant poison exactly as had the husband of her own fictitious creation, Ina Hart.

"Absolutely impossible," she repeated aloud.

The compulsion came to go to Albert's room, as though seeing the place where Albert had died could provide her with some knowledge about his death. The door opened easily, silently. The blankets were huddled over the foot of the bed. The sheets were gone; evidently the police had for some reason taken them.

Abruptly, a feeling of loss overcame her. That Albert had

been Albert made his ending pitiful. A small busy man, absorbed in his job. A man of shrewdness, of pride, of tact, who had suddenly and without dignity gone the way of beggars and kings. "Oh, Albert," she whispered, and felt tears start to her eyes.

A sound startled her, the sharp sound of metal striking against cement. She turned her head toward the north window. The sound seemed to come from there.

Neatly framed by yellow curtains, an old man was standing at the edge of the driveway of the big house next door, which was perhaps two feet higher than the narrow side yard of her own house. A low white picket fence hid his feet, but she could see that his gnarled brown hand was clasped loosely about the handle of a garden spade, which had made the ringing, metallic sound she had just heard. His head was craned forward on its leathery old neck, and below the brim of a battered felt hat his faded blue eyes met hers squarely with the unconscious impertinence of intense curiosity.

She recognized him as the gardener who at Christmastime had handed her a bunch of poinsettias over the same fence. But there was no friendliness on his face today. He had smelled death.

Anger burst in her. With three sharp strides she reached the window and violently drew the curtains together, their metal rings clashing against the rod from which they hung. She found that she was panting in the dimness of the bedroom. The sound of her own breath coming and going reminded her of the breathing of an animal at bay.

The doorbell rang. It rang again before she realized that

Hazel was not there to answer it. It was with reluctance that she went down the little hall ending at Albert's door, turned into the wider hall where the telephone was. For the first time she could remember, she went to her own door with a sense of dread of what might be waiting there.

It was a messenger boy. He was chewing gum. He matter-of-factly handed a long green florist's box over the lower half of the door. She set it down on the dining-table to open it. Inside were two dozen long-stemmed red roses, her favorite flower. A small white envelope was pinned to the clear green wax paper which had covered the flowers. A white card was inside.

*Happy Birthday, Victoria. Sawn.*

*Chapter Six:*

## THE LABEL THAT WASN'T

TUCK WAS admitted to the inner office of George Leighman by a secretary so exquisite she almost succeeded in awing him. Mr. Leighman was growing both heavy and gray. He had anxious eyes. It took him some time to absorb the fact that Albert Hime was dead. "But, my God," he exclaimed, slapping his balding forehead, "he was going to produce *Ina Hart.* Everything was all straight except the signing of the contract!" From the window Tuck could see part of an outdoor set. The sails of a very Dutch windmill turned idly in the California sunlight.

As to the matter of the possible poisoning of Mr. Hime from something he had eaten in the café, Mr. Leighman was most positive. "Ridiculous! All he had was a cup of black coffee. I saw him drink it."

"And you were with him the entire time?"

"No. My car was at the garage here being checked; I'd rid-den in from Culver City with him. Lester, Miss Hastings's agent, offered to drive me home. Wanted to talk about Hastings, of course."

"So Miss Hastings and Mr. Hime were alone after you left."

"Alone?" asked Leighman. "There were about a hundred other diners packed all around them, if you call that alone."

"Is there any possibility, in your opinion, that there was something more between Mr. Hime and Miss Hastings than a business association?"

"If a producer got into a lather over every pretty blonde who walked into his office, he'd be in a lather all the time," commented Leighman.

"There's just one reason why I ask. In my long talk with Mrs. Hime this morning, it struck me that she was a woman of unusual intelligence, and at her best of unusual brilliance of personality. And Mr. Hime slept in what had been the guest room. It struck me that the ego of the husband of Mrs. Hime might suffer a little. I wondered if Miss Hastings, because she would be inclined to look up to Mr. Hime as a power in her world, might have become a means of escape from a certain sense of inadequacy his wife gave him."

Leighman said, "Not the slightest hint of that has leaked out." He added, "Hime was lucky to have Victoria for a wife, and he knew it. She's a remarkable woman." His broad, worried, clever face contracted into a frown. "Poor Vicky," he said. "Poor little woman." He reached for his telephone. Tuck left him with a pantomime good-by. He was speaking blundering words of comfort to Mrs. Hime.

The secretary of the agent, Louis Lester, consented to give Tuck Moira Hastings's address. He found her apartment without trouble. It was one of those pretentious white stucco places called "Chateau This" and "Villa That" that rear themselves proudly against the backdrop of the low hills above Hollywood. Repeated knocking at the white door bearing her name brought no response.

He went next to the café, whose name he had obtained from Mr. Leighman. After a talk with the manager, the night waiters, who had just come on duty, were lined up. An intelligent-looking elderly man with very flat feet remembered having served the table where Albert Hime had taken the black coffee. He remembered because he had recently seen Miss Hastings in a featured role in which she reminded him of his young daughter Marcia.

At that hour the spacious restaurant was almost empty; the waiter led Tuck to the semicircular glassed-in booth where Hime, Leighman, Hastings and the agent Lester had been seated the evening before.

No, the small dark man had taken nothing but one cup of black coffee, like the bald older man in the gray suit. Both had explained late dinner engagements when they gave the order. The other two, the actress and the slim guy, had had roast beef—a regular meal. Yes, the slim chap and the older man left together. How long did the actress and the handsome dark fellow talk together after the others left? Not over ten minutes; he himself had seen to that; it was part of his job to keep patrons from dawdling. No, he had no idea what they had been discussing. The actress sat there tearing up the lace-paper doilies the restaurant had been using since the laundry trouble. Every time he looked over that way to see if she was through with her meal so he could present the bill, she was tearing another doily into small pieces. The scraps had lain all over the table like confetti when he cleared away.

No, after the others left the dark man didn't eat or drink anything. He left alone. When the waiter went to reset the table, the actress told him she was waiting for her escort, who would be back shortly. When he asked if she would mind waiting in the large entrance room because so many people were lined up for tables, she was short with him at first and then was very pleasant, said she understood. As she slid out of the booth something dropped to the floor and he picked it up; it was a manuscript bound in that black paper that looks like leather. She took it with her. It was evidently a play or something called *Ina Hart*. He remembered the name he saw on the cover because he found the same name written in pencil over and over again on the only doily she had not torn up.

When Tuck tried Moira Hastings's apartment again an unusually pretty amber blonde answered the door and admitted that she was Miss Hastings. When he identified himself, she retained the expression he had seen on the faces of daughters of very rich men. It was a look of insulation, as though its owner placidly accepted the fact that the slings and arrows of outrageous fortune would never be her lot. When he entered the characterless, expensive living-room of the apartment he saw that she had been shopping. There were two large boxes on the sofa from one of which spilled the red of a dress she must have begun to unwrap when he rang the bell. "I can't imagine what you want to see me for," she said, as she pushed the dress into the box and replaced the lid. He told her that Hime was dead.

She straightened from the box and looked at him as though she was about to accuse him of lying. Then she doubled at the knees and fell forward, still with that look of protest on her face. Her fall pushed over the coffee table before the sofa and a pile of *Time* magazines spilled to the floor. She lay huddled on the thick gray rug, the faces of several newsworthy people staring up around her lovely profile. Her forehead had struck the corner of the little table sharply, and as he lifted her and carried her to the sofa, pushing the two boxes to the floor, he could already see the faint pinkish beginnings of a bruise on the front of the photogenic skull.

When she came to, she stared up at the ceiling, then looked at him. She said in a muffled voice, "Call my agent, Mr. Lester." Then she began to sob.

"There were several questions I wanted to ask you," said Tuck, "but they can wait until tomorrow."

With her hands still covering her face, she nodded emphatically, and he left her lying so.

As he closed the front door he reflected that if she had staged the faint she had not picked her spot very well. He also reflected that with what Leighman and the waiter had already told him, there was little Miss Hastings could add, except to tell him what she and Hime had discussed during the ten minutes after the two other men left, and perhaps why she had torn up all those doilies.

For one fact was abundantly clear to him, and indeed he had not expected that it would turn out otherwise. Albert Hime had not been poisoned just before he returned home.

He then telephoned the studio and got Mr. Hime's secretary. Her reaction to the news of his death was the same unbelief Leighman had shown. Rather dazedly she gave the information that Mr. Hime had eaten a tray lunch sent to his office by the commissary. It had consisted of a combination salad and a cup of coffee. She had eaten the same lunch herself, without ill effects. That, thought Tuck, seemed to leave either a slow-acting poison which had been ingested before the day he died, or the single remaining inescapable fact that whatever had poisoned Albert Hime had been eaten during or shortly after the little supper his wife had prepared and served. The autopsy would tell which was the case.

He telephoned the City Hall. Froody told him that the autopsy had not yet been made, nor had the report from the chemical laboratory come through. Tuck bought a dollar copy of *Ina Hart* at a cut-rate drugstore and read it with considerable interest, which rose to a crescendo when he learned that its author was fully cognizant of the extremely lethal properties of sodium fluoride, which had composed the chief ingredient of the ant poison in the small, dusty package which Froody had found from the top shelf of the cupboard in her den. He had since discovered that a small amount of this poison, about three to four teaspoons, had been at some time taken from the contents of the box, at least if the statement on the label as to the net contents told the strict truth.

### Hollywood Producer Dies of Poison

*While his wife slept peacefully in another bedroom, Albert Hime, 38, died early yesterday morning. The family physician, Dr. Joseph Mahler, was called by Mrs. Hime when she went to arouse her husband at a little after seven in the morning and found him dead. Dr. Mahler ascertained that death had come as a result of poison. He at once called the police.*

*Mrs. Hime is Victoria Jason, film writer and novelist. She could not be interviewed because of her shocked condition but the police reveal that she is at a loss as to any possible explanation of her husband's sudden demise. The police are at present working on the theory that poison was administered to the dead man accidentally. The body has been removed for autopsy.*

*Mr. Hime's film career began as director of early musicals. Prior to coming to Hollywood in 1932, he directed and produced two musical comedies on Broadway. He was at this time the husband of Della Fagan, the cough-syrup heiress. She obtained a divorce from him in Reno. His most recent production was a mystery film, "The Cold Boy." He was to have produced the film version of his wife's novel, "Ina Hart." He was born in Chicago, but has been since 1932 a resident of Southern California.*

Later, Victoria wondered how she had been so blind. She wondered if horror closed in on all its victims as it had closed in on her, swiftly, unexpectedly, like a trap snapping shut. And not long after that, she wondered at her blindness on another score. Traps are set. Where there is the trapped, there must also be the trapper.

But on the second morning after Albert's death she awoke

with her blindness still upon her, and with the sound of the ringing telephone in her ears. She knew that it would probably be the first of her fifty intimate Hollywood acquaintances who, having read the morning paper, had called to offer sympathy, aid and curiosity but thinly disguised.

She was right in her guess. Standing barefoot on the cool floor of the little hall, she heard the voice of Leonard Hermes, a brilliant and erratic writer who had once fancied himself in love with her. His outstanding characteristic, in addition to what he confessed to be genius, was a very large nose. He had once told her, sullenly, that only a man with a large nose and the superabundance of intelligence which always went with a large nose would ever be capable of appreciating her strange charm.

"My sweet," he said, as always, "my sweet, this is truly dreadful. What can I do?"

"Not a thing, Leonard," she said.

"There must be something. There is something. Are they persecuting you? Do you need a friend? I am your friend, Victoria. You know that."

"Yes, *my* friend. You are my friend. But really, there isn't anything anyone can do."

The amenities disposed of, Leonard went to the point with an alacrity which, in one of lesser genius, could only have been labeled as naive. "I am of course consumed with curiosity. The papers—have you seen them?—are most indefinite. They mention poison, and say the police are conducting an investigation—why do the police always *conduct* an investigation?—but what I of course want to know is every little grisly detail."

"You'll have to wait for tomorrow's paper, then. I'm pretty much in the dark myself."

"Oh," said Leonard, flatly.

"Anything else?" asked Victoria.

"Do you want me to come over to be with you? I'm working on a ghastly thing out here, and should be charmed to let my collaborator fritz it around by himself for the day, the rat."

"That wouldn't do any good, Leonard. I would really rather be alone."

Very cheerfully he said, "Just as you say. And Victoria—I was right, wasn't I?"

"About what?"

"Albert, as I recall him, had a *very* small nose. Did you find him genuinely *sympathique*?"

Victoria quietly broke the connection and then removed the receiver from the hook until Hazel should arrive to take over. She became aware of the same emotion which had gripped her when the old gardener stared into Albert's room the day before—the sensation of being at bay.

Lieutenant Tuck arrived an hour later, after she had put on an unbecoming dark blue dress. The morning was gray. Seeing him standing so huge in the doorway, Victoria was aware of him for the first time as a menacing figure. There was a passive threat in so much size pitted against the wrongdoer. As he stepped into her house, she saw that his attitude toward her had undergone a subtle change. He looked down at her in a puzzled way, as a man looks at some strange animal of which he has heard but which he has never seen. They went to the living-room and took the same places they had occupied the day before—she on the sofa, he in the chair facing it. The script of *Ina Hart* was gone from the coffee table now; evidently Hazel had removed it.

"I'm going to ask again a question you answered no to yesterday. Was there anyone who might have had a reason to murder your husband?" Tuck asked.

"No."

"Yesterday you mentioned in passing that you had had certain visitors in the afternoon and early evening. Who were they?"

"Moira Hastings came for tea at about four. She stayed perhaps an hour and a half. Then my friend Mrs. Saxe dropped in at six; she was upset over a private problem and wanted to discuss it with me. At about seven a Captain Harriss arrived unexpectedly. He stayed for perhaps three-quarters of an hour. I had to leave to pick up Albert, and when I returned Captain Harriss had gone."

"Who is this Captain Harriss? A friend of yours, or your husband's?"

"Neither. He was my first husband. We were divorced ten years ago."

"Then he didn't know Mr. Hime at all?"

"He'd never seen him."

"And those were your only three visitors?"

"Yes."

Tuck was silent for a minute, looking at the coffee table as though he were reading something on its dark surface. Then he looked up at Victoria and she noted irrelevantly that the sockets of his eyes were outlined with flesh a little darker than that of the rest of his face, which gave him a weary look. He said, "The autopsy has been made. Your husband died of a lethal dose of sodium fluoride. The poison was found in the stomach and large intestines along with the remnants of the last meal he ate. This means that the poison was ingested not more than half an hour before or after that meal. It was not taken before; witnesses have testified to that."

That was when Victoria had the first sharp sense of a trap closing about her. "You mean that he was poisoned in this house, at dinner?"

"He must have been."

"But that's impossible."

He looked at her with that puzzled, curious look. "My assistant, Mr. Froody, in searching your den, found a box of ant powder pushed far back on the shelf of the closet. This had been at some time opened. Some of the poison had been removed."

As he spoke, recollection smote Victoria like the lash of a whip. Controlling a desire to expostulate, to rise and pace the floor and speak loudly and defiantly, she said, "My explanation of that poison is going to sound thin. It happens to be true. A year ago I began work on *Ina Hart*. It involves murder by poison."

"I know," said Tuck.

"I asked Dr. Mahler for the name and properties of a poison which would not act for about six hours. He let me read a book on poisons he has in his office. I picked sodium fluoride. The book said it was the chief basis of most commercial ant powders. I had to know whether it was necessary to sign the poison register when you bought it. To find that out, I bought a box. I also had to know whether it was soluble in water. I used a small amount of the powder to find this out. It did not entirely dissolve in cold water. I tried it in milk and coffee. These were better; they hid the milky look of the dissolved powder, and the dregs which did not dissolve. Why I didn't throw it away I really can't tell you. That cupboard in my den has been a catchall for odds and ends for a long time. I put it far back on the top shelf so no one could get into it accidentally, and then I forgot it. I just simply and plainly forgot it, Mr. Tuck. I had not thought of it again until you mentioned it just now."

"And your servant didn't come across this box of poison and ask if you wanted it? In a year's time?"

"Hazel has strict orders against tidying my den. Ever since forty pages of final draft vanished into the incinerator."

Tuck again looked at the coffee table while he thought. His next remark puzzled Victoria. "I seem to have the notion from something you said yesterday that you are on a diet, and are using no sugar."

"That's right."

"I also seem to remember that your husband used two spoonfuls of sugar in his coffee."

"Yes, he did. Albert is terrifically fond of sweets."

"That's what killed him," said Tuck quietly.

She stared at his long solemn face. She jumped to her feet

and walked to the center of the room, from where she could see the sideboard in the dining-room. The silver teapot and the coffee pot and the creamer were there on the tray, but the silver sugar bowl was gone.

"I took it downtown with me yesterday," said Tuck. "I learned from Hazel that was the bowl which was always used on the dinner table. I thought I noticed something wrong about that sugar when I lifted the lid and looked into the bowl. I took it to the police chemist. He recovered about six teaspoonfuls of sodium fluoride. This had been mixed casually in with the top sugar, so that anyone using sugar from that bowl would pick up about fifty percent poison."

The morning sun completed its struggle with the mist and glowed sudden and warm through the orange curtains just at the moment that the realization of how Albert had come to die burst through the fog of her puzzlement and glowed in Victoria's brain. She felt her certainty shining on her face as she said to Tuck, "I know how Albert died."

She took a step toward him as though physical nearness could emphasize what she was going to say. She realized that for the first time she was looking down at Mr. Tuck. "My servant Hazel keeps a large quantity of ant powder in a can in the kitchen. It is between the one containing salt and the one containing sugar. A month ago she reached for the wrong can and filled the sugar bowl with salt. When she filled that sugar bowl this time, she made the same mistake, but in the other direction. She filled the bowl with the poison, Mr. Tuck."

"Mighty careless," was Tuck's only comment.

"It was the carelessness born of trusting too much to habit. I've watched her at work in the kitchen from time to time and she reaches for the canister she wants without really looking at it. She reached for the wrong one again."

Tuck rose. "I'd like to have a look at that can of poison." There was something guarded in his voice.

They crossed the black-and-white squares of the kitchen linoleum together, he in three heavy treads, she in five short ones. The commonplace, everyday look of the room itself, of the row of identical green canisters on the sideboard was infinitely reassuring. Tuck's big hand closed on the can between the one labeled sugar and the one labeled salt. He pulled up the lid, which left the can with a faint, hollow twang. He stood looking down into the can and then tilted it toward Victoria. Its bright tin interior was empty.

She took it from him and turned it around. The red-edged label reading *Ant Poison* which Hazel had pasted to its side was also gone. *Tea* said the black letters now. There was nothing to indicate that the can had ever contained poison.

The moment of silence was broken by the sound of the service door opening at the far end of the room. Hazel entered, carrying a brown bag of groceries against her flat little chest. She smiled at Victoria and said, "I found some dandy corn, dear. Small kernels, like you like." Her gaze then shifted to Tuck and then to the green can Victoria was still holding.

"Hazel," said Victoria. "What happened to the poison that was in this can?"

"It just ran out, dear. I used the last of it a week back."

Victoria continued to stare at her. Hazel added, as she came forward, "I noticed it was gone last Saturday, just after you took Haggis to the vet's to be spayed."

The calm, absurd irrelevance of the event which placed this fact in Hazel's mind had a curious quality of finality to it. Victoria took the lid Tuck was holding, replaced it on the can, put the can back in its place between the others. She could feel Tuck looking down at her. She felt her throat constrict as she swallowed.

Outside, in the sunlight, a bird sang merrily.

*Chapter Seven:*
## STUMBLING IN THE DARK

IT WAS midafternoon. Tuck, Froody, and Gufferty, the head of the Homicide Squad, were gathered around the polished expanse of Gufferty's large flat desk. From the street outside the proud white building traffic noises came to them faintly. It was the time of day when the office workers in the building knocked off for a coke, a cup of coffee, or to buy an apple or a candy bar from the old lady who had for years had a stand in the echoing mouth of the Main Street entrance. The three men looked tired but absorbed. When Tuck finished speaking, Gufferty put both hands to the sides of his round, balding head, rocked it gently from one side to the other. Then he swung his round body suddenly and dangerously back in his swivel chair. Lying back so, he rubbed the round spot in the center of the circling tonsure of graying hair like a man rubbing an ache.

"It is the damnedest case I've ever heard of," he announced. "It's like a damned storybook murder." Gufferty seldom swore.

"It is," said Tuck. "However you look at it, the basic pattern remains the same. A woman writes a book in which the central character poisons her husband; the woman's husband is then killed with the same poison."

"Things don't happen that way," said Froody.

"Once in a million times they do," corrected Tuck. "It would seem that we are face to face with the once-in-a-millionth time. Let's accept that and go once more over the facts we have. To begin with, we know this: Hime was killed either by his wife or by one of the three people who visited his wife on the afternoon of the day he died. There is no apparent motive for any of these four people to have killed him, so for the present we'll consider opportunity instead of motive. The opportunity can be boiled down to this: Miss Hastings, Mrs. Saxe, Captain Harriss, and Mrs. Hime herself all had the opportunity to place the poison which killed Hime in the sugar bowl. The bowl was filled by the servant Hazel the night before, after dinner. It was not again used until four in the afternoon, when Miss Hastings and Mrs. Hime had tea together. Neither of them used sugar in their tea, according to Mrs. Hime. The bowl was then returned to its usual place on the sideboard by the friend Mrs. Saxe, where it remained until Mrs. Hime herself set it on the dinner table, which was at about seven, just before her first husband paid his unexpected call. There it remained until Mrs. Hime and her husband cleared the dinner table, at which time she returned it to the sideboard where I found it the next morning.

"Now. After Mrs. Hime had somewhat recovered from the shock of learning that there was no ant poison in the kitchen

canister, I went over all the events of the day before in minute detail. I have a notebook full of minute details. She hasn't
been eating, she was knocked out, she sat on the sofa in the
living-room smoking cigarettes, she walked up and down the
room. She seemed to want to talk. I know every moment of
that rather full Thursday afternoon. I could not help noticing
that each of those three visitors had the physical opportunity to put poison into the sugar unknown to Mrs. Hime. She
was called away to the telephone during Miss Hastings's visit
and remained there talking long enough for the act of poisoning the sugar to have been committed. And Mrs. Saxe was
left alone for about ten minutes while Mrs. Hime changed her
dress, and the first husband, Harriss, was alone in the house for
a possible half-hour while Mrs. Hime was driving her husband
home.

"If one of those three visitors, for an unknown reason, put
poison in the sugar bowl, that person had poison with him
when he entered the house. The reason is clear. Neither Miss
Hastings nor Harriss had been there before and could not
possibly have known of the box of poison in Mrs. Hime's den."

"Mrs. Saxe could have known," said Gufferty.

"There seems a chance of that, yes. But she could not have
got at it without attracting the attention of Mrs. Hime, who
was dressing in the bedroom which opens directly off her den,
where the poison was.

"Now granting that one of those three persons entered the
house armed with poison with which to commit murder, there
are three alternatives. This person intended to kill Mr. Hime,
Mrs. Hime, or both of them.

"And here's where the whole thing becomes illogical. Let's take each of these three people one by one. Moira Hastings did not apparently know of Mrs. Hime's diet. Therefore, if she poisoned the sugar, she must have wished to kill both Mrs. and Mr. Hime. Would she want to kill the producer through whom she hoped to get a fat part? It seems to me impossible to consider for even a moment.

"Bernice Saxe. She knew Mrs. Hime was not using sugar. If she put poison in the sugar bowl, she intended to kill Albert Hime. She went to that house with poison in her purse to kill her best friend's husband. There is not the slightest inkling of any possible motive.

"Captain Harriss. Even more impossible. When he went to Mrs. Hime's he did not know she had a husband! Therefore, to qualify as the murderer, he must have gone there armed with poison with which he meant to kill Mrs. Hime. *But* he learned she was not using sugar. So would he have then poisoned the sugar in the bowl?"

"Are you sure Harriss and this Mrs. Saxe knew Mrs. Hime was not using sugar? I mean, she may have mentioned it in passing, but they may not have been listening," Gufferty said.

"I checked that point carefully with Mrs. Hime. They knew. Mrs. Saxe herself brought up the matter of the diet. Mr. Harriss mixed some old-fashioneds. Mrs. Hime asked him to leave sugar out of hers, and told him that she was watching her weight. The next drink he brought her was without any sugar; he had heard, all right.

"I said there were four people who had an opportunity to put poison in the sugar. There were really five, the servant Ha-

THE BIRTHDAY MURDER · 91

zel having had an opportunity to do so the night before when she filled the sugar bowl. And Hazel also knew Mrs. Hime was not using sugar. Setting aside the glaring lack of any motive, does it seem likely that she would have chosen to murder Mr. Hime by a method which put so many lives in danger? It was just chance that the sugar bowl was not used during the day, before Mr. Hime took that fatal sugar. And furthermore, would she choose a method which could be traced so directly to her?"

"It seems to me," said Gufferty, "that you've sealed, signed and delivered a case against Mrs. Hime."

Tuck sighed heavily. "Now we'll look at that. Again we have to assume some strong motive, of which there is absolutely no indication. For some reason, then, Mrs. Hime desired to get rid of her husband—"

"Insurance?" suggested Gufferty suddenly.

"Out. Mrs. Hime made about three times as much money as her husband did. He carried no life insurance policy for this reason."

"Just wanted to get it straight," said Gufferty.

"For some reason Mrs. Hime wanted to get rid of her husband—"

"Maybe something about this Hastings dame? Jealousy," Gufferty said.

"Maybe. So Mrs. Hime carefully chooses the same poison she had a character in her last book use in killing her husband. She leaves roughly a pound of this poison in her closet. She puts the poison in a sugar bowl which will be used by Hime at a dinner where only she was present. She then takes a sleeping pill, sleeps for about eight hours, awakes in the morning, finds him dead, calls the doctor. She exhibits, according to a talk I had with him by phone, all the usual signs of shock. But even granting that these were faked, and that the woman is a hard-souled murderess, would she have been likely to commit this murder in that way?"

"Murder in passion," said Gufferty. "Maybe there was a sudden flare-up—she's raging. Before she thinks about the consequences, she's gone and done the thing the way her own character did it."

"Except that poison does not go with a murder committed in passion; it takes some sort of plan to use poison. It takes coldness, and cruelty, and a scheme."

"Well, no sudden passion then," acquiesced Gufferty. "She has been simmering for days, maybe weeks. She's found her husband is being unfaithful to her with the actress." Gufferty rubbed his head excitedly. "Wait! I think I have something here. She's got a plan, and a good one. She poisons her husband in a way that right off throws suspicion on her, but she doesn't care. She's counting on that poison in the kitchen! She's going to maintain that the servant did it accidentally! If she sticks to that, there's no way we can disprove it. The servant would deny it, but who wants to admit to such a mistake? Mrs. Hime sits tight. She's got money, she's got a lot of friends. The case against her begins to look fantastic even to us. Against her doing it is the simple explanation of accident on the part of the servant. You know as well as I do what the verdict at the coroner's inquest would be. Person or persons unknown. Hell, maybe the jury would even find the servant guilty of negligence. Maybe we might suspect justice hadn't been done, but how could we prove it?"

"Except," said Tuck, gently, "that if this had been Mrs. Hime's plan she would have certainly made sure that the poison in the kitchen was there, since her neck depended on it."

Gufferty deflated. "Yeah."

"Well," said Froody, "it seems to me you've proved no one could have killed Mr. Hime."

"But someone did," said Tuck, "which means that our facts are wrong."

"Or maybe your interpretation of them?" put in Gufferty, slyly.

Froody cast a bulging look of distaste at Gufferty, and began to count out facts on his pudgy pink fingers. "One: Hime died of sodium fluoride. Two: From the sugar bowl. Three: Five people had the opportunity to put poison in the sugar bowl, and yet that's only technically; as soon as you boil it down it sounds ridiculous."

With a malicious grin Gufferty, like a prestidigitator, drew from his drawer a sheet of blue-ruled notebook paper of the type found in children's five-cent pads. "Came in this afternoon's mail," he said. On it was written, in a crotchety and feeble handwriting: *Albert Hime did not die of poison. I killed him by Remote Control. The Godless shall Perish. I have been chosen for This Work.* It was signed *George Washington Bliss.*

Tuck had handled five cases involving killers who had committed crimes in passion. Three of these were Negroes. All three, after the knife had slit, or the razor, had waited quietly with the body for the police to arrive. He never forgot the Negress who had fatally slashed her husband. He had arrived at the small drab house to find the corpse lying on its back on the floor, a bloodstained pillow under the head, the wife sitting in a chair beside the body, rocking gently from side to side. Seven neighbors were grouped in the shadows of the little room, as silent as the furniture itself. He never forgot the curious dignity with which the woman rose and looked up at him out of her brown eyes with their yellowish whites. "Ah done wrong. Now Ah'll take mah punishment."

Two of these killers had been white. One was a middle-aged woman who had shot the youth for whom she had formed a passionate and yet maternal love; the other a carpenter who had struck his wife repeatedly over the head with a hammer. In these two there had been at the core the same sick unhealthiness of a mind turned in on itself, gnawing on its resentments.

Long before these experiences, Tuck had given up the romantic notion that in one mad moment a human being may take another life, having been before and becoming afterward a normal man or woman, the victim of an inner storm. He knew that murder in passion, like any murder, takes long years of preparation during which a human mind goes through a complicated evolution necessary to bring it to the point when murder can be done. What so troubled him in regard to Mrs. Hime was the fact that she was totally unequipped to commit a murder in sudden passion. She had apparently none of the weak self-engrossment which was a primary requisite, lacking that complete maladjustment which the Negroes had suffered from. She was not a woman to brood over trifles, because she was too busy. Her life had been one of enlarging opportunities, created by herself out of her own talent and effort.

Such a woman might still be capable of cruelty, given sufficient provocation—of which there was no sign here. But there he ran against the snag of her intelligence. Planning a crime, she would certainly have planned a better one.

He recognized this stage of the case as the hardest of all; the stumbling-in-the-dark period which would be terminated by some sudden new fact or some twist of the old ones, but took patience to get through. He decided to begin by finding whether anything revealing or unusual had occurred during that ten minutes Hime and Moira Hastings had spent together in the glass booth of the busy, glittering café.

This time Moira Hastings was not alone. She had on a severe black slack suit with a short little jacket, white ruffles showing at throat and wrist. On her feet were black espadrilles. Her face was very pale; since the smooth flawlessness of make-up covered it, he could only decide that she had dressed her face also out of respect to the dead man, choosing a paler powder than the ripe, golden tone she had worn the day before. The black suit was like a costume; she was like a character from some sleek drawing-room tragedy, wearing trousers after death to assert her modernity, but choosing dull black wool and wistful white ruffles out of a certain nicety of taste. He noticed her clear, light eyes, which made him think of some semiprecious stone whose name at the moment escaped him.

In the unlived-in living-room, Tuck found a slim, well-dressed and exceedingly self-possessed man of indeterminate years seated on the sofa pretending to look over the most recent issue of *Time*. He laid the magazine aside and stood up as Miss Hastings and Tuck entered from the hall. "This is Mr. Lester, my agent. Louis, this is Mr. Tuck. He's from the Homicide Squad."

Mr. Lester came forward to shake Tuck's hand with a small, tense hand full of energy. They all sat down, facing one another. Mr. Lester offered a pack of cigarettes with raised brows, was refused, lighted one for himself and said through a first exhalation of blue smoke, "A bad business."

Moira Hastings was sunk deep in a large armchair in what Tuck knew at once was a favorite attitude. Her long slim legs were extended, her chin was down among the ruffles of her white blouse, her red-nailed hands were clasped over her flat abdomen. "He means Mr. Hime's death," she said to Tuck.

"Yes," said Mr. Lester. "I mean about Hime. Terrible thing. For him of course. But for Moira here, too. It looked pretty much as though he was going to toss her the lead in his new picture."

"Which is hardly relevant," said Moira.

Lester stared at her out of protruding eyes in which there was a look of wonder. Then he looked at Tuck.

"You can see," he said, "why she needs an agent. Someone has to look after her. She's got the stuff. She's got the talent."

Moira's head with its aureole of amber hair tilted back on the long throat. She rested the crown of her head against the back of the chair and smiled a little. "He's trying," she said, "to give you the impression that I'm a flowery and sensitive little thing. I'm not. I know that Mr. Hime's death did me out of the biggest chance I've had yet in this damnable town. But I liked

Mr. Hime. So now his death concerns me more than its effect on me. Later, I suppose, I'll get around to feeling bad about the part I might have had."

"See what I mean?" asked Mr. Lester of Tuck. "Artists. I've known hundreds, of 'em. All the same. You take the common run of women, and they'll think of themselves first every time. But an artist is different. She gets a different angle on the situation. She'll always surprise you with a different angle." He finished, triumphantly, "That's an artist for you."

"Shut up, Louis, and let Mr. Tuck talk," said Moira, calmly.

Beginning with a statement which always sounded very foolish to him, but which invariably seemed to satisfy the person to whom he made it, Tuck said, "First tell me a little about yourself. I always like to know something about the background of a witness."

This time it didn't work.

Moira Hastings's eyes widened. "But I'm not a witness to anything," she said.

Tuck nodded. "Correct. I used the word loosely."

Once this matter was disposed of, the universal desire of all people to talk about themselves launched Moira Hastings into a short biography. He learned that she had been born in Los Angeles in 1920, that her father was a local hardware dealer, that her mother had insisted on dancing lessons for her from the age of four. She starred in the high school senior play, went for a year to junior college and majored in dramatics. The woman dramatic coach had taken a violent dislike to her, and so gave all the leads to a girl of inferior talent. Moira Hastings changed to the Pasadena Community Playhouse, where she worked up to leads from bit parts and painting scenery. There she was discovered by a talent scout, was given a small part in a picture and a short-term contract. "He was one of the kindest men I have ever known." But her option was dropped in six months. At that time she became affiliated with Louis Lester, who got her a number of parts, finally her contract with her present studio. Through him she met Mr. Hime at the studio commissary. She had known him about five months at the time of his death. He was one of the kindest men she had ever known.

"During that ten minutes or so you spent talking to Mr. Hime on the evening of his death, did you notice anything unusual about him? Did he say or do anything out of the ordinary?"

"No. He was a little edgy; I knew that was because he was not yet absolutely certain that Mr. Leighman would give him the opportunity he wanted. To do *Ina,* I mean. I was sure of it, and told him so. But you know how it is with some people: when they want something very much they're absolutely certain that they aren't going to get it. It's a form of knocking on wood. Then they have all the fun of being excited and surprised when it happens. I think that's what Albert was doing."

"Albert," put in Mr. Lester quickly, "was the only producer for the job."

It did not escape Tuck that he had sought to cover Miss Hastings's use of the dead man's first name with the same familiarity on his own part.

"What exactly did you talk about?"

"The picture. That's all we ever talked about, ever since he first learned he might do it and started to consider me for the part."

"This may seem rude. How did he come to consider you in the first place? I mean, you're very young. His wife seems so certain that an older and more experienced actress should do it."

"Mr. Hime saw me do the wife in *The Animal Kingdom* at the Playhouse four years ago. Of course, he didn't know it was me, then, but he remembered how good I'd been. He was convinced that if as a girl of twenty-one I could play a woman of thirty-five, and do it well, I could play Ina."

"And she could, too," said Louis Lester.

"So you discussed the new picture at the café." Tuck leaned forward. "Why," he asked solemnly, "did you tear up all those paper doilies?"

Moira Hastings's head drew back a little on her long throat. She stared for a moment at Tuck as though she disliked him very much. Then she smiled. "I always tear things up. It's one of my little habits, isn't it, Louis?"

"One of her little habits," repeated Lester, looking full at Tuck and nodding his head emphatically.

"And now about Mrs. Hime," Tuck said. "Did you notice anything unusual in her behavior when you had tea with her on Thursday afternoon?"

"I had never met Mrs. Hime before, so I couldn't really say," said Moira Hastings carefully. "The first thing she said when she met me at the door was, 'But you're terribly pretty, my dear.'

"What I really went up there to see her about was the part. Mr. Hime had told me quite frankly that she was against my getting it. I got thinking, and decided that after all she'd probably only seen me as that gushy schoolgirl Clarissa. I felt, in my innocence, that if I did a scene from *Ina* and showed her I could handle something more mature, she'd withdraw her objections. I realized that she had great influence on her husband, of course." Her voice became hard. "But it didn't work out quite that way."

There was calm authority in her tone when she said, after a brief pause, "It didn't take me long to realize that Mrs. Hime was hideously jealous of me."

Louis Lester said, quickly and brightly, "Oh, come now, Moira. Those are very hard words. I am sure Mr. Tuck won't—"

"She was jealous of me," said Moira Hastings, implacably. Tuck remembered the name of the jewel of which her eyes had reminded him. Aquamarine.

Her voice became more casual. "I don't think Mrs. Hime actually realized this. She thought that what she called my inexperience was her real reason for being against me." She brooded on this for a moment, and then sat up in her chair. Leaning forward toward Tuck, her small hands gripping the arms of the chair, she said, "I've read several of Mrs. Hime's stories, in addition to *Ina Hart,* and I've noticed a funny thing. A very funny thing." She lowered her voice so that it was only a whisper. "She hates beautiful women. In all her stories it is the pretty women who have the black hearts. In back of their faces there is always something twisted and dangerous. Something wrong."

Louis Lester's voice was loud, bright, and angry. "Moira

took some freshman psychology once, and she never got over it," he said.

Moira Hastings's head turned toward her agent in a snakelike movement, smooth and deadly. Her lips closed thin over what she wanted to say to him.

Tuck stood up. Lester stood up. Slowly, Moira Hastings stood up. She spread her fine slim hands out helplessly at either side of the slenderly curved hips in the slim black trousers. Her eyes looked up at Tuck. She was giving herself to his approval for an instant. Then she dropped one hand loosely at her side and jammed the other into her trouser pocket. "Oh, what the hell," she said, easily. "I don't hold it against her. I've had it before, and I'll have it again, jealousy from women."

After the white door had closed after him, Tuck stood outside Moira Hastings's apartment, listening. He could just hear Lester say, "For God's sake, Moira! Keep out of this! It'll ruin you! I already told you that!"

There was a silence. Then Moira Hastings spoke in a choked voice. "She killed him, Louis. I know it."

The house where Mrs. Saxe dwelt was painfully bisymmetric. It presented a bland, square, cream-colored façade to the late afternoon sun which blinked on the glass of the windows, each with its neat striped awning. From the exact center of either half of the deep and slightly terraced front lawn a tall palm tree shot upward, its thin naked trunk circled at the base by a bed of extraordinarily large pansies. A wide cement walk bisected the lawn, led uncompromisingly to the oaken front door with a triangular window of heavy glass. A cement porch ran the width of the house; on either side of the steps dwarf orange trees stood in large cement urns.

Mrs. Saxe herself opened the heavy door. She looked only a little taken aback on seeing him, and at once became the hostess. She ushered him into a living-room notable for the rich stolidity of all the larger pieces of furniture, an effect somewhat tempered by such whimsies as mirror picture frames, gay bric-a-brac, defiantly charming odds and ends of color which he guessed to be expressions of the personality of Mrs. Saxe. They did not quite conquer the heavy and unimaginative magnificence of the room.

Tuck sat in a massive upholstered armchair which welcomed him grudgingly. Bernice arranged herself in a similar chair, half facing him. Between them was a little round table on which a Dresden china shepherdess offered pink roses in her upheld skirt.

"I suppose it's something about Mr. Hime's death?" said Mrs. Saxe. "I really don't know a thing about it, not a thing."

"I came to ask you a few questions about Mrs. Hime," said Tuck.

"About Victoria?" asked Mrs. Saxe, somewhat overdoing her surprise. He saw that there were dark shadows under her eyes, and wondered why.

Mrs. Saxe's discourse was rambling, breathless, incoherent. She spoke rather sentimentally of childhood days together, girlhood days at a New York high school. From what she told him Tuck got the feel of the relationship of the two women and saw why it had lasted down the years. From the first they had been necessary to each other. The clever girl had needed the less intelligent one; the pretty girl had needed the plain one. Although each by contrast had underscored the other's lack, she had underscored the other's virtue, too, and this had been the more important to the growing egos. Victoria's brilliance as a student had shone against Bernice's slowness; Bernice's success at dances, with young men, had been paraded before her friend.

Victoria had been maid of honor at Bernice's first wedding, a very lavish one. When Victoria married Sawn Harriss they had eloped to Wilmington, Delaware. In speaking of the breakup of Victoria's first marriage, Bernice said how shocked she had been, how grieved for Victoria; her brown eyes moved in her face, her mouth moved, but nothing concealed the fact that the catastrophe had offered Bernice gratification.

In marrying a young man both wealthy and handsome, Victoria had stepped out of character as the career woman who might achieve her own lonely successes, but not the security and dignity of marriage which Bernice had attained. That Victoria should have had at 24 the editorship of a small magazine, and a potentially rich young husband as well, had disrupted the nice balance which had characterized the relationship of the two friends. That Sawn Harriss turned out an impossible young man had seemed to Bernice Saxe almost inevitable, Tuck saw.

All this was interesting, but irrelevant. Then, in speaking of Victoria's divorce, something splashed out of the steady stream of Mrs. Saxe's words which caught Tuck's attention. "Of course, I've always thought that the sale of her first novel really tipped the scales. I mean, as far as the blonde in the shower went. Sawn was a crazy one, and Victoria knew that, and she was crazy about him and they might have made it all up. But Victoria's a funny person. She gets worked up to a certain pitch of excitement and then she's apt to do anything. And when she walked in and found the blonde, she'd just got a phone call down at her office when she was working late, that her first book had sold. On top of all that elation, she had cold water dashed into her face, and I've always believed it set her a little crazy. Otherwise she'd never have hit him and left the apartment and then gone to Reno the next day. Of course, that's just an idea of mine."

A telephone bell rang in the depths of the house. In a moment a stout housekeeper with a cold face came to the door leading to the hall. "Mr. West," she said.

"I'm not in," said Bernice Saxe, coolly. Tuck thought that he saw color in her cheeks, however, a luster of suppressed excitement. There was also, as she settled back in her chair, an air of disappointment in her pose. He felt an intruder, watching her. For a moment her attention was turned inward on some troubling private matter, the same worry, he guessed, which had put the dark circles below her eyes. She turned her head and looked down at the little Dresden china shepherdess offering the pink roses in her skirt. A peculiar intensity came into her look, as though she were seeing more than the figurine.

Tuck said, "One final question. When you saw Mrs. Hime shortly before her husband came home, did she say anything that would lead you to believe there had been trouble between them? Was she upset?"

Bernice looked straight at him and for the first time her eyes were without their girlish sparkle. They looked dead and old. "Oh, no. She was in high spirits. She'd just learned that her first play had been taken for Broadway production."

"Did Mrs. Hime ever say anything to you about Moira Hastings?"

"Albert's little protégée? Have you seen her? I never have. She's awfully pretty, isn't she? Blonde?"

As Tuck went down the cement walk, deep in thought, the air felt different on his head, and he found he'd forgotten his hat. He returned and rang the bell; the somewhat grim house-keeper opened the door at once. He picked up his hat from the gilded console table beside the door and as he did so heard Bernice's tiny, light voice call from the living-room, "Oh, Mrs. Buxton. You'd better get out the dustpan. I've broken the little Dresden shepherdess."

As Tuck closed the door after him Mrs. Buxton's voice came woodenly. "What a shame. Mr. Saxe always liked that piece so much."

With the idea of talking to the third and last of Mrs. Hime's visitors, Tuck set himself the task of finding Captain Harriss. Since he had apparently made the trip from wherever he was stationed in order to see his ex-wife, whom he had known to be living near Hollywood, he had undoubtedly stayed in Hollywood or near it, and unless he had visited friends a check of the hotels should turn him up.

Tuck's fourth phone call brought results. Captain Harriss was registered at the Hollywood Roosevelt, on the Boulevard.

He had given as his address Camp Roberts, which Tuck knew to be near San Luis Obispo. He was not in his room. Hanging up the phone, he reflected that Captain Harriss had come a long way to call on a woman he had not seen for ten years.

His mind veered to Bernice Saxe, to her voice calling to the housekeeper about the breaking of the Dresden shepherdess. He wondered why that troubled him. Then he remembered that the figurine had been standing in almost the center of the small table. It would be impossible to brush it off to the floor accidentally.

Why would Mrs. Saxe choose to break that innocuous china lady?

The owner of the house next door to Mrs. Hime's admitted that the party he had on the Thursday in question had been very loud indeed. He admitted this smilingly, as a tribute to himself as a successful host.

As Tuck drove his black sedan down the sloping street to Sunset Boulevard, he reflected that Victoria Jason Hime's reason for taking a sleeping pill on the night her husband had died had been validated.

A small gray convertible coupé, the top down, passed him, going up the hill. He recognized Mrs. Hime at the wheel, dark glasses on her face, her gray hair more wind-blown than ever.

There had been a party next door. But in Mrs. Hime's house there had been black silence, and a woman sleeping a drugged sleep, and a dead man in another room.

*Chapter Eight:*
## CHALKY STRIP OF DEATH

THE DOG Haggis was a small energetic Sealyham, whose earnest brown eyes peered up through a fringe of grayish-white hair, whose entire hindquarters collaborated whenever she wagged her tail, which was often, and who labored forever against a rapacious hunger. Victoria was aware of a certain similarity between herself and her little dog. "We're just a couple of elderly girls," she sometimes said to Haggis.

The veterinary telephoned shortly after Tuck left on Saturday afternoon. Haggis had quite recovered from her operation and might be called for whenever convenient. This lifted Victoria from the fog of puzzlement which had descended on her when she learned of the absence of any poison in the kitchen canister. She realized that the unnatural silence of her house was due largely to the absence of the bustling Haggis, and she knew that the return of the dog would do a great deal toward raising her spirits.

Driving back from the vet's, with Haggis's cold moist nose

against her bare ankle, Victoria's spirits rose. She turned into her street from Sunset with the baseless feeling that somehow everything was going to be all right.

Smiling, Victoria entered her house. Hazel was bustling about the sunny kitchen. But the smile left Victoria's face when Hazel said, "Bernice called, dear. She wanted me to remind you that you had better make arrangements about Mr. Hime's funeral."

So Victoria went to the phone and called the undertaker whose establishment stood in simple stucco grandeur at the foot of her street.

"I think, Mrs. Hime," said the man's soft voice, "that you will have to come down and select the casket."

"Oh, you can do that all right, I'm sure," said Victoria. "Just something simple and expensive with silver handles."

"We do not usually do it that way, Mrs. Hime. We have a very large selection of caskets, and it has been found to be better for the deceased's kin to make the selection."

So Victoria reluctantly prepared to leave the house on a most unwelcome errand. Just before she left, Hazel asked if she might have the rest of the afternoon off, as it was the only time she had been able to get an appointment to have her hair waved, and Victoria acceded to the request. "I'll be back in time to serve your dinner at six," she promised.

When Victoria returned home and let herself in with her key, she went into her bedroom and put on one of her two black dresses. In the den she stopped and looked down at the yellow page still spilling from the roller of her typewriter. She wondered if she would ever finish that page, if the pressure of the strangely unreal reality of the last two days would ever ebb and allow her to step into her private world again.

She went to Albert's room and selected his best dark suit, the one he used for small dinners, and laid it across the bed. She would take it later to the mortician's. She wondered what she would do with the rest of his clothes, and decided to send them to the Red Cross. She telephoned, and they said they would send up a truck on Monday. She forced herself to go through all the pockets. She found the stubs of two theater tickets for a show they had seen a month before; two partly consumed chocolate bars, half a package of cigarettes, a fountain pen. On the lapel of one suit was a dark red smudge of lipstick.

Dolefully she went out of Albert's room and closed the door tightly after her. She called for Haggis, but Haggis was not within earshot. She left the front door open so Haggis could get in.

Hazel called at 5:30 and said she had been delayed. Victoria told her there was no hurry, that she wasn't very hungry. Then she decided that Haggis might be, and opened a can of dog food. She put some in Haggis's blue bowl, which Hazel had thoughtfully left clean and shining just inside the service door of the kitchen. "O.K., Haggis!" Victoria shouted. "Food now!"

But the call which usually brought Haggis bouncing excitedly into the kitchen had no such result. Victoria decided that Haggis was after the cat again, and went to the front door and called from there. No Haggis. She went partway down the steps leading to the graveled driveway and called again. Then she saw the gray Persian cat stretched in luxurious content atop the whitewashed wall that separated the long driveway from the old orchard which flanked the house on the south. She was licking one limp paw idly. Victoria knew that this was a piece of trespassing Haggis never permitted, and turned back to the house with worry at her heels. Could Haggis's short absence have made her lose her old familiarity with the house and its environs? Could she have wandered far afield and got lost?

Ten minutes later she found Haggis. She found her on the small walled balcony, lying half under the long sun-chair. Her eyes were closed and her little belly was rising and falling with her quick breathing. When Victoria stooped down beside her, Haggis opened brown eyes to look once at Victoria, and then closed them again. She touched the dog's nose with one forefinger. Dry and hot. Its usual shiny blackness was gone; it looked dusty and unwholesome.

She gave the dog's shaggy head a quick soft pat and stood up. With strides amazingly long for so small a woman, Victoria launched herself toward the telephone. She looked up the number of the veterinary, dialed it swiftly, and to the man's voice which answered she said, "You just spayed my dog. You send someone up here fast. She's very sick. You've botched something badly."

"Oh, I hardly think that's likely. We—"

"I don't give a damn what you hardly think! This dog is dying, and I am holding you responsible!"

"Who is this talking?" asked the man.

She told him, and gave him the address.

"We've really closed for the day," said the man, "but I'll

come up myself. Keep perfectly calm, Mrs. Hime. It is probably just some minor postoperative reaction which—"

"Don't talk like an ass! I've seen the dog. There's something terribly wrong with her! You get here fast!"

With an inarticulate sound, the man broke the connection.

When the doorbell rang twenty minutes later, Victoria was squatting once more beside Haggis, softly stroking the panting, shaggy side, whose rise and fall seemed now even more rapid, more indicative of the death spreading through the little animal's body.

The veterinary had not stopped to change the high-necked and impressive white coat which all the attendants wore on duty. An anxious crease was between his brows, and he was carrying a small black bag not unlike a doctor's. "Where's the dog?" he asked tersely. She led him to the balcony. He squatted down beside Haggis, his big clean hands going swiftly over the dog's body with professional gentleness. Under the pressure of his fingers the dog gave a sudden choked cough, ducking her head as a human being does. The big hand went almost tenderly up to Haggis's throat and pressed. Haggis gave another cough, and a thin watery substance spurted from her mouth, falling with a wet flat sound onto the flagstones.

The veterinary looked up over his white-clad shoulder at Victoria. His face was no longer anxious, but set and remote. "This dog has been poisoned," he said.

The vet took Haggis with him. He believed he could save her. Victoria paced up and down the living-room, full of the fear which had filled her on the morning of Albert's death.

Once more, poison without reason. Who would poison Haggis? But who would poison Albert? Her husband and then her dog—

She stabbed out a cigarette on what she saw a moment later was fortunately an ash tray. She forced herself to think coherently. Somehow Haggis had eaten poison since returning home. There did not seem much likelihood that it could have been accidentally eaten. Although Hazel had once put a strip of the powder along the outer sill of the kitchen service door, Victoria had warned her against doing so, because of the chance that Haggis might lick some up.

Victoria thought over what she knew about dog poisoning. The most usual methods were to mix poison with ground hamburger or place some in a slit in a piece of meat, and leave the poisoned food where the animal could easily find it.

A complete circuit of the yard surrounding the house revealed no trace of any meat, although that did not mean much, because Haggis might have eaten all of it. Victoria combed the ivy that covered the front yard, but found nothing. A search of the oily floor of the garage was equally fruitless.

She went up the wooden steps leading to the service door. Standing on the little porch between the utilitarian trash box and the equally utilitarian garbage pail (which the luxuriant bougainvillea vine concealed from view from the front), Victoria allowed herself a moment to look toward the west. She turned, put out her hand to open the kitchen door, looked down, and learned how Haggis had been poisoned.

At her feet, pale in the cool gray-yellow light, a strip of chalky white powder extended along the weathered gray boards of the porch, just below the doorsill. She bent over it. The tiny dead black bodies of several ants were imprisoned in the powder. Just below the corner where the door opened, and against which she had so often found Haggis pressing her little black nose while she barked to be let in, there was a three-inch gap in the strip of poison. Peering still closer, Victoria could see the drool of drying saliva where Haggis's hungry tongue had licked at the white strip. A vivid cerise flower with three triangular petals fell from the vine above her head and landed just beside the gap between poison and poison.

Automatically, she looked up. Through the interstices in the vine the blank twilight sky stared back. And then the vine whirled above her head, and she stood up slowly and carefully, her brain spinning. Spinning, but steadily and with balance, like a top set into motion by expert hands and whirling so perfectly it seems to be standing still.

There had been no poison along this doorsill when she took Haggis to the vet, a week before. She had left the house by this door, and there had been no poison. Hazel had said that the poison in the kitchen canister had run out the day Haggis left for the vet. How, then, did the poison come to be below the doorsill now?

The conclusion had been in her head since the moment she had seen the strip of poison. There must have been poison in that canister after Haggis had gone. Hazel had used some of it in laying this trap for ants.

Hazel had lied.

A car entered the driveway beyond the porch and then stopped. In a moment the door slammed. A footstep sounded hollowly on the bottom step. Victoria turned and looked down at Hazel, who plodded the rest of the way up the steps to where she stood. Victoria looked down at the strip of white at their feet, looked at Hazel. Hazel was staring at the poison as though mesmerized by that pale white line in the last daylight. When her eyes behind the thick glasses met Victoria's they wore the furtive look of guilt.

It was Victoria who opened the door. She stepped into the house, Hazel at her heels. She snapped the switch beside the door, and the kitchen was flooded with hard, revealing light from the white globe overhead. She turned to Hazel and noted that her ears, bared by the close crimping of her hair at the hands of the beautician, were very pink. Hazel blinked once in the hard light as some small, trapped animal might blink. She said, "I'm sorry to be so late. Are you hungry?"

Victoria was conscious of the need for proceeding carefully. She was aware for the first time of something unstable and fearful in Hazel, and saw her not as what she had always seemed to be, a little, matter-of-fact, elderly woman. She saw her as a person who had at one time possessed a life of her own, a person fated by some inadequacy to clean other people's homes, cook their food, wash their dirty dishes, pretend to like them.

"The poison in the green can didn't run out last Saturday," Victoria stated rather than asked.

The furtive look drained from Hazel's eyes. She shook her head in lengthy negative, as a child does. "No."

"When did you put that poison out on the porch?"

"The day before Mr. Hime died. Wednesday morning."

"What really happened to the poison?"

"I threw it out. I emptied it into the sink and washed it down the drain with hot water. I took the label off the can, too."

"When?"

"Friday morning. While you were asleep on the sofa."

"Why?"

Hazel's eyes widened a little as though she thought this already known. "Why, because the police were coming! Because Mr. Hime died from poison!"

Victoria stared at her.

"Don't you see?" Hazel asked.

"I don't."

"Why, it was to make things all right for you, dear. The police would have jumped to conclusions, maybe taken you down to jail."

"Where did you get such an idea?"

"Mrs. Saxe told me."

"Bernice told you that?"

"Well, not in those exact words. You see, she got here a little after I did. We were both very excited and upset. After she covered you with a blanket she came in and we talked about Mr. Hime dying from poison. Dr. Mahler told us on the phone. She looked over and saw the label on the can and said, 'Oh, dear, I wish that stuff weren't here!' I asked her why, and she said Dr. Mahler had phoned the police. She said she didn't have much of an opinion of the police, from all she'd heard. She said they seemed to jump to conclusions. I said, 'You mean this poison being here might make them think there had been something funny going on?' She said yes. She said they might get ideas. She said you were her best friend and she knew you wouldn't hurt a fly, but the police didn't know that. I said, 'We could throw it out,' and she got quite excited and said, 'Let's do that. It can't do any harm.' So I did. While I was scraping the label from the can those first two policemen rang the bell, and Mrs. Saxe stood at the door waiting until I nodded to her to open it. Then, when they'd gone to the bedroom to look at Mr. Hime, we whispered together a minute and she said not to say anything about it to you, that you were a bad liar.

"I'm a good liar," Hazel added cheerfully. She seemed much happier to have got her secret off her chest.

"Yes," said Victoria. "You are."

*Bernice,* she was thinking. *Is Bernice quite so stupid as that?*

Victoria was pulled to her friend by the strong pull of curiosity. She had to know something. She had to try to judge whether Bernice's desire to eliminate the poison from the kitchen had been simply a manifestation of hysteria, or whether there had been a more concrete reason. Whether Bernice, for a short while at any rate, had been able to believe that she could have killed her husband.

She telephoned Bernice. With Walter's car gone she was stranded; that's why she hadn't been past, although she'd phoned innumerable times on Saturday. Victoria told her the receiver had been off the hook for quite a while.

"Darling!" Bernice expostulated. "They arrest you for that! Or at least take away your phone."

"It was Leonard Hermes. He happened to be the first person to telephone, and after talking to him I decided I didn't want to talk to anyone I knew."

"Even me?" asked Bernice, with teasing reproach.

"All except you," Victoria forced herself to say.

Before she left for Bernice's she telephoned the vet's. He assured her that Haggis would live.

The housekeeper, Mrs. Buxton, always retired to her room at the rear of the house at eight, unless there were guests expected. Mrs. Buxton had come with the house, which Walter had inherited at the death of his mother, and had her prerogatives. Looking through the lace-curtained triangle of thick glass in the oak front door, Victoria saw Bernice coming down the curved staircase which graced the large hall. She moved lightly for a tall woman growing heavy, and her hand slipped almost caressingly down the wide mahogany banister. She was wearing lounging pajamas of pale green satin.

Seeing her so, Victoria was reminded of something, she could not remember what. Something or someone infinitely familiar, as familiar as Bernice herself, of whom Bernice in that moment reminded her.

The oak door squeaked just a little on its hinges as it always did. It was a rich squeak, a permissible squeak, a squeak for which no apology had ever been made. Bernice's tiny voice welcomed Victoria warmly. But she herself did not look warm. She was paler than usual, and the icy color and texture of her garment made it seem as though Bernice should shiver as she spoke. "Come up to my room," she said. The two women went up the thick carpet of the stairs in silence. Ever since she had taken Stanley West as a lover, Bernice had believed that Mrs. Buxton listened behind doors.

Bernice's room was the dream-room of an eighteen-year-old schoolgirl. Bernice was the only woman Victoria had ever known who actually possessed a white satin chaise longue.

Bernice curled herself into the chaise longue, Victoria took the softly floral slipper chair. She was aware for the first time of a strangeness between them. A direct approach to the matter of the destruction of the poison was for some reason impossible to her. She asked Bernice if there had been any word from Walter.

"I called him at the lodge this afternoon," said Bernice.

"Oh? Do you think that was wise?"

"I'm not a very patient person; I like to get things over with."

"Is everything all right?"

"Everything's fine."

"I'm very glad, Bernice. Walter's really an awfully nice guy."

"You see," said Bernice, "I'm going to have a baby."

"You're—!"

"Oh, I don't mean I *am* having one. I mean I've decided to."

"Oh."

"It's something Walter's wanted for a long time."

Victoria was silent.

"I explained to him that I'd done a lot of thinking about the matter of Stan. I explained that I didn't admire the man at all, and so I couldn't really account for what had happened.

I explained that I'd decided that this strange thing with Stan was really a hidden desire for a child taking that form—Stan *is* a child, in many ways." Bernice smoothed the arm of the chaise longue with one finger. She looked up at Victoria out of candid eyes. "And you know, Vicky, I'm sure what I told him is quite true."

Victoria could think of nothing at all to say. Over and over in her head a silly phrase kept singing itself. *Beware of Greeks bearing gifts.*

"How has Stan taken your change of heart?"

"Nobly," said Bernice, with dryness. She giggled. "He has bravely given me up, because my happiness is so important to him. He will make his lonely way as best he can, smoking his pipe and wearing white shirts open at the neck in even the coldest weather."

Victoria laughed with her.

"Really," Bernice said, wiping the tears of her laughter from the corners of her eyes, "women are so strange. We do such strange things. I don't understand us at all. I don't understand myself. I—"

Victoria seized the lead this comment gave her. "I've been thinking much the same thing," she said. "Why in God's name did you talk Hazel into throwing out that ant powder?"

The soberness and stillness that came over Bernice was startling, after the relaxed way in which she had discussed two matters of such vital importance. "Oh. How did you find out about that?"

Victoria told her. "And then Hazel said that it had really been your idea."

Bernice said, "I was really beside myself that morning, Vicky. I mean, the day before all that mess with Walter, and then this terrible thing happening to you."

"For a person beside herself you managed to carry the thing off with quite a lot of dispatch."

"I felt that I had to, for your sake, Vicky."

"How for my sake?"

"Because I thought you'd used some of that poison to kill Albert."

Even though she had foreseen this possibility, the words shocked Victoria to the bone. She found herself on her feet. "This is incredible!" she said loudly.

Bernice was sitting stiffly against the small pillows now. "Is it? Think of the state I was in that morning. Think of what I'd just been through with Walter. Remember I knew, Vicky, that you and Albert had eaten alone there the night before. Think of Sawn. You remember that. You remember how you behaved over that silly little blond thing he brought home. I thought of that actress. And there was Albert dead, and there was all that poison."

Victoria sat down and fumbled in her purse for a cigarette, which she lighted. Bernice waited until she'd taken a first puff, and then went on: "I mean, I don't think so now, Vicky. I've had time to cool down and think it over. But then, and for just a few minutes, I was *certain* that you'd learned something about Albert and this young actress, and that you just went berserk. I don't mean anything cold and calculated; that wouldn't be you, Vicky. I mean just dumping poison into something he would eat or drink the way a person pulls the trigger of a gun. And of course, in back of your mind would be the knowledge that the ant poison was deadly because of *Ina Hart.*"

"I'm very tired of that name," said Victoria.

Bernice jumped up from the chaise longue and came to Victoria's chair. She bent down beside it, dropped her arm over Victoria's shoulders. "You're not angry with me, are you?" she asked, imploringly.

"No," said Victoria slowly, not looking at her friend. "I'm just thinking how little we know each other, Bernice." She got up, roamed the room looking for a place to stab out her cigarette. Bernice came forward with a white china ash tray. Victoria extinguished the burning tip of her cigarette thoroughly. "You don't know me at all, and I'm afraid that I don't know you either."

"You know me like a book," said Bernice lightly. "You certainly proved that the other night."

Like a book. The phrase again stirred that odd sense of similarity in Victoria's brain. Something Bernice reminded her of.

"I want to use your phone," Victoria said.

"Who are you calling?"

"The police, of course. Mr. Tuck."

"You mean to tell him about the ant powder?"

"Yes."

Bernice jerked a step forward. "Do you think that's the best thing to do?"

Recalling the dusty box of ant poison found in her den cupboard, Victoria said dryly, "Decidedly so."

Bernice took another step forward. "Vicky. I wouldn't call from here. I'm *sure* Mrs. Buxton listens on the downstairs phone."

Victoria put down the receiver. Bernice said, "It'll make me look a dreadful fool. Whatever shall I tell them when they come and ask me why I did it?"

"The truth," said Victoria, standing up. She suddenly wanted to get out of that large, flounced, satin room.

Bernice looked her shock. "Oh, no! That'll look so bad for you!"

Victoria was on the point of telling Bernice that nothing could look as bad for her as the absence of the poison had, but something stopped her. Again she was aware of that estrangement which now lay between them.

"I'll simply say I was hysterical," said Bernice, "and wasn't really responsible."

Then she froze into an attitude of listening. Victoria heard the sound of the big oaken front door closing. "Walter!" breathed Bernice. The approach of a lover never lighted such delight in a woman's eyes.

Victoria drew on her pigskin driving-gloves, put on her short gray fur jacket and went down the silent carpeted stairs.

In the hall below, Walter was just kissing Bernice's lips. He was a spare man, not very tall, and his thinning hair was combed carefully to hide incipient baldness. "Hello, Walter," Victoria called, and the man and wife broke apart.

"Well, well," said Walter. He always reserved a humorous smile for Vicky, as though they had both at sometime agreed that there was something vaguely funny about a woman who wrote for a living. They shook hands. Victoria knew that Walter was probably quite aware that the situation which had sent him away from his home was no secret to her, and that this embarrassed him greatly. He stood a little in front of the pigskin bag he had set down as though hoping to conceal the fact that his absence had been an unusual one.

Bernice's arm was twined through her husband's. She was looking almost adoringly at his profile. "Doesn't Walter look darling with a tan?" she asked.

Hideously at a loss for an answer, Victoria was glad when Walter broke almost brusquely from his wife's grasp to take off his overcoat. "Scarcely 'darling,'" he said in his careful, lawyer's voice.

"Nice to see you again, Walter," Victoria told him and turned and went to the door. Bernice turned her head to say, "I'll ring up tomorrow, Vicky. Don't worry about anything. Everything will be all right."

"I'm sure it will," said Victoria. She was not referring to her own problem.

As she shut the heavy door, she could not help looking back through the glass triangle. Walter was putting his coat away in the hall closet, settling it very precisely on a hanger. Bernice was watching him intently. As he turned toward her, shutting the closet door in the same motion, she went toward him, holding out her hands.

As Victoria went down the cement walk toward her car, she heard the high fronds of the palm trees whispering sibilantly far above her head. She was suddenly full of that troubling sense of a likeness between Bernice and someone else which

had come first when she saw Bernice gliding down the staircase of her husband's house, her hand caressing the banister,
and which had edged into her consciousness again when Bernice watched Walter's back while he hung his coat away.

Bernice had reminded her, in those two actions, those two
instants, of Ina Hart.

Which was ridiculous, because no two people could be
more unlike.

Victoria at once qualified that. The two women did have
one thing in common. They had been trained to regard men
as creatures whose primary function was to provide them with
what they wanted. But Bernice, Victoria reflected with a rather
grim smile as she slipped in under the steering wheel, had not
killed Walter, which had been Ina's method of removing one
corner from an equally dangerous triangle.

Ina was a destructive personality. Bernice was not.

## Chapter Nine:
## MRS. WATT HAS HER MOMENT

TUCK HUNG up the receiver thoughtfully. What Mrs. Hime had just told him changed everything. That was his first thought. Then he paused to question its validity. How? Well, first and foremost, since the poison had been in the green kitchen canister after all, Hazel could have made the mistake which Mrs. Hime had advanced as explanation of Albert Hime's death.

Hazel Bennett lived in a small and scrupulously neat furnished apartment with a canary and three fan-tailed goldfish. She seemed almost eager to tell Tuck of the part she had played in the destruction of the poison. When he said gravely, "You must realize that the destruction of evidence is a crime, punishable by law," some of the brightness faded from her face.

She said, in a crumpled voice in which there was some fear, "But I didn't think of it as a crime when I did it, Mr. Tuck!" as though that statement exonerated her, and against such feminine logic Tuck had long ago learned not to do battle. She added, "And anyway, it wasn't my idea!"

"But you were thinking of the mistake you made with the salt a month ago, weren't you? When Mrs. Saxe convinced you that the police always wanted a quick arrest, you remembered that mistake you'd made before, and you were afraid for yourself."

Hazel's soft face stretched into a look of astonishment. "I never even thought of it!" she said.

"It was you who filled the silver sugar bowl that was used on the dinner table," said Tuck.

"Yes. I filled it just before I left on Wednesday night."

"And you realized that since you'd made one mistake, with the salt, you might be accused of having made another, with the ant powder."

Hazel sat up straighter. "I never did!"

"You could have made just that mistake, though."

"No!"

"How can you be so sure? An accident is a slip; it happens unconsciously. The mind can't be positive about it."

Hazel was eager once more. "But I couldn't have! Don't you see! I'd reached for the wrong can just a little while ago. You don't make the same mistake twice, so close together. The first mistake keeps you on your toes! Like there's a place out front on the pavement where the roots of a tree make the sidewalk stick up in a crack. I fell over that place a couple of months ago. Now I watch for it! I walk around it!"

Tuck had to concede the validity of Hazel's psychology for all the simplicity with which she worded her idea.

She went on hurriedly, as though by talking she could keep him from further unpleasant suggestions. "When I first got those canisters about a year ago I thought, 'You'll be getting them all mixed up if you don't watch your labels.' Such a silly thing, really, to make them all the same size. Anyone knows you don't need nearly as big a can for tea as you do for flour. Most of those sets are in different sizes, going from a little tiny one for pepper up to a great big one for flour, because that's bulkiest. But I had to take what I could get when I bought them. I was lucky to get those. I remember I said to the hardware man, 'A man made those. And he's never been inside a kitchen.'"

Tuck took advantage of a pause for breath to say, "You are willing, then, to swear under oath to the fact that you could not possibly have put ant powder into the sugar bowl, instead of sugar?"

The words "swear under oath" seemed to have a sobering effect on Hazel. She regarded Tuck out of her pale eyes behind the thick lenses of her glasses. Then: "I'll swear to it."

Tuck stood up. At the door he turned to look down at her. "Didn't you realize that if you destroyed the ant poison in the kitchen there was still the ant poison in Mrs. Hime's cupboard?"

"In her cupboard?"

"In that shallow closet in her den."

"But I didn't know about that! I never laid eyes on it!"

He opened the door, and turned to ask, "Could Mrs. Saxe have seen it?"

"Mrs. Saxe? I suppose she *could* have. She was in and out a lot, and Victoria always leaves doors and drawers open." Then Hazel's face brightened. "No! She couldn't have! Because if she'd known about the poison in the den, she'd have wanted to get rid of that too!"

Froody lived in a small, neat bachelor apartment on a street that sloped up from Westlake (now MacArthur) Park. It had been there for as long as Tuck could remember, surrounding a shallow turgid lake on which ducks, a few white swans, rowboats and little mud hens swam. The lake was entirely circled by green-slatted benches on which people sat by day for the reasons which prompt people to sit on park benches.

When Tuck's knock at his friend's door brought no response, he knew that Froody was either at the movies or walking around the lake. Tuck had become adjusted to the flat smell of the water, the damp smell of the grass, when he saw Froody's dumpy, unmistakable form walking slowly ahead of him. He fell into step; Froody showed no surprise. Their familiarity with each other's ways explained Tuck's having found him.

Tuck told about Mrs. Hime's discovery concerning the ant poison.

Froody removed from his mouth a briar pipe as short and stubby as himself and asked, "And Mrs. Hime told you that Mrs. Saxe got rid of the poison because she thought she—that is, Mrs. Hime—might have killed her husband with it?"

"She did."

"Hm. Now it doesn't seem to me she'd say that, if she really did kill him. Does it to you?"

"No. Unless she realized that it would sound better coming from her."

Froody looked doubtful at this subtlety. "Yes. There's that." He thought a minute. "Of course, the fact that this Hazel is willing to swear that she didn't put ant powder in the sugar doesn't prove a thing. That's the last thing she'd want to admit, when she has to make her living as a housekeeper."

"True," said Tuck.

"So at one end we have two alternatives: Hazel did or didn't. And at the other end there's two more: Mrs. Hime did or didn't. And both of them have a mighty good reason to say they didn't. So we can't believe either of 'em."

"And then," said Tuck, "there's the middle. The other three people who had as good an opportunity to poison the sugar as either Hazel Bennett or Victoria Jason Hime."

"Only no motive," reminded Froody.

"No known motive," said Tuck.

From the bench they were passing a girl said, "All right, Harry."

"But aren't you changing all around?" asked Froody cautiously. "Last time we talked about these people you washed 'em out complete and utter."

"That was when I believed the murderer had to bring his poison with him. But now it was in the kitchen, waiting for him. All he had to bring was himself. Himself, and a certain psychological setup within himself of which we don't yet know. It may have been the sight of that green can with its red-edged poison label that brought the plan for murder into being in his brain."

"It *sounds* good," said Froody. "Only who? And why?"

"Well, once more Miss Hastings drops out. She wouldn't kill the man she hoped to get that part from."

Froody took the pipe from his mouth. "What if she meant to kill *Mrs.* Hime?"

"Would she choose a way which would kill him too?"

Froody put the pipe back into his mouth without comment.

"That leaves Saxe and Harriss," said Tuck. "The old friend and the first husband."

"And he'd never set eyes on Hime."

"That's right."

"And she doesn't seem to have had anything against him, does she?"

"No."

"What does the fact the poison was right there in the kitchen do to Mrs. Hime's story?"

"I can't see that it changes it much. If you argue murder in passion you still have the whole character of the woman to contend with; if you argue premeditation you have the presence of the ant poison in her cupboard to contend with. It's conceivable that she may have forgotten it if she's innocent, but if she's guilty, the use of the poison in the kitchen would surely have called it to mind, and she'd certainly have destroyed it before we got on the scene."

"Yes."

"Of course, if you want to argue that she was going to rely solely on an accident on the servant's part to clear her own skirts, the fact that the poison was in the can in the kitchen all the time does allow that."

Tuck was aware that he spoke grudgingly.

"You don't *like* to believe Mrs. Hime did it, do you?" said Froody.

Tuck laughed a little. "Put it this way. You know how leery I am of circumstantial evidence of the sort we're facing here—where everything seems to point to one conclusion. Well, from the very start, so many things have pointed glaringly to Mrs. Hime that I find myself fighting the conclusion that she did it. When a conclusion is being slowly forced on you by someone you're arguing with, it gets your back up; you try hard to refute it."

He let his voice trail off, and the two men continued to circle the black little lake in slow silence. The last words he himself had spoken echoed in Tuck's brain. "When a conclusion is being forced on you."

A rowboat's oar splashed on the lake; the sound of a kiss came from the darkness to his right. A queer notion edged into Tuck's brain. That he was meant to arrest Victoria Jason Hime for murder. That someone had intended this. That Albert Hime had been killed that this might come about.

He shook his head. Fantastic. What did he know, what really did he know to support such a conclusion?

Nothing. Bernice Saxe was, to his knowledge, a slightly stupid woman who had known her friend Victoria for almost 25 years. Harriss was not even a face. He was a blank in the uniform of an Army captain who had returned out of Mrs. Hime's past to talk with her of old times on the same evening that, unfortunately, her husband died of poison.

Concerning Captain Harriss, a phrase lingered in his brain.

From somewhere, a phrase. Spoken in a small, high voice. Oh, yes. Mrs. Saxe's voice. "He was a crazy one."

He decided he wanted to see and talk with Captain Harriss, to fill in this annoying blank. He returned to Froody's apartment to use his telephone. They heard it ringing as he opened the door. Froody answered it. A look of interest glowed on his cherubic face. He replaced the receiver. "That was Gufferty. There's a woman down there named Mrs. George Watt who says she has important information about Mr. Hime. About his death."

Mrs. George Watt was sitting very straight on the edge of one of the hard chairs in Gufferty's office. She was a small, plump woman, clad in what was obviously her best. Over a black dress the top of which was ornate with gold studs set in a rather ugly design she had on a fur coat of brown lapin a little worn at the cuffs. Her black hat, small and rakish, had a great deal of veiling. On her well-powdered cheeks bright rouge gave her a look of hot excitement. She *was* excited, Tuck saw at once.

Tuck took her to the small private office behind the larger one opening from the marble corridor, and they sat in two brown leather chairs. Mrs. Watt's purse started to slide from her short, sloping lap, and she grabbed for it with a little scream, and then rested one hand on her bosom and gasped, "I'm so on edge!"

She took the cigarette which Tuck offered, puffed inexpertly while he lighted it for her.

"Mr. Gufferty tells me you have some important information about the death of Mr. Hime," he said.

She nodded. "We were once husband and wife," she announced, with quiet drama. He saw that she had thought carefully over the words she would use to tell this, had chosen those.

Tuck waited.

Mrs. Watt, seeing that this information did not electrify him, took a second and more successful puff on her cigarette, and said, "So I thought that you might want to question me."

"I see. You were married when?"

"In 1925. We went to the same high school. We were—well, sort of sweethearts. I went on to business school and got a job as stenographer in a packing house—this was in Chicago—and he worked in the packing shed. He was saving enough money for college. We got married at the end of his freshman year."

"What made you come here?"

"Well, the girls at the club I belong to were having our annual dinner—we always do that, every year. We go to Chinatown, oh, twenty of us, and have a grand dinner, and then we go to an early show. We're a bridge club. Well, at dinner one of the women mentioned the death of a producer named Albert Hime, and how she thought the wife must have done it from what she'd read in the papers. Well, right away I knew that must be my Albert. Not only from the name (it's an odd one) but from the fact that he was always so interested in that sort of thing. In college he directed a lot of student plays. I went to them and they were certainly good—real deep stuff, you know, by people like Shaw."

Tuck nodded encouragingly.

"Well, all through the show—Bette Davis, my, she's wonderful—I kept thinking of Albert, and him being dead, and what this friend of mine had said about the wife doing it. After the show we went to the 'Pig 'n' Whistle' for sodas and sundaes, and so then I told the girls about how I had been married once to Albert. My, they were excited. Then I asked them whether they thought I should go to the police and offer to tell all I knew about Albert, being married to him once, like I say, and they all thought it was really my duty and so I decided I would. I came right straight here, because I knew if I waited and got thinking it over and talked about it with George, I'd never in this world come. George is so cautious. Several of the girls offered to come down with me, but I didn't let them, because I knew they'd just be in the way. Hetty Corcoran—she's been president for four years running—was *green*. She always likes to be the whole show."

Mrs. Watt, Tuck saw, had had Her Moment. "And what do you know of Mr. Hime that might throw some light on his death?" he asked.

Mrs. Watt drew herself up very straight. "Just this," she said. "His wife didn't kill him."

"How do you know that?"

Mrs. Watt deflated just a little as she sought for reasons. "Well, I *know* Albert. I mean, we were married almost three years altogether, and he's not that sort of man. I mean, for someone to kill you, you've got to have something wrong with you. Unless a woman's stark, raving crazy, she doesn't just go and kill her husband without any reason. In fact, no one kills a person without any reason. Albert was—well, he didn't have a mean bone in his body. You just couldn't get mad at him. He always made you feel like a queen. 'Stick with me, Glad,' he'd say, 'and you'll be wearing diamonds and drinking champagne by the bucket.' He was always wanting to do nice things for you. Of course, he didn't have any money then, none at all. He used up what he saved from the job at the packing plant for tuition and books and all at the University. We just had my salary and a little he picked up from a Saturday job as a sales-man, but out of that little bit of money he always saved out enough to bring me something nice—a bag of candy, or a gar-denia—*something*."

"Still," said Tuck, "you did divorce him, didn't you?"

Mrs. Watt's eyes looked back over the years. "You know how young girls are. I was crazy for pretty clothes, and it made me awfully mean sometimes. Albert always pointed out that if I'd just be patient until he finished college and got a start I'd have these things, a lot more than if I had just married one of the boys at the plant who'd spend the rest of their lives slaughter-ing pigs for a living. But I was impatient and selfish, the way girls are. I used to get worked up at him. He was always so pa-tient, always saw my side of it. The divorce was my fault, really. I'd kept telling myself that if I could stick it out until he grad-uated, I'd get my reward. But then he just went on at the store as a full-time salesman. Of course, I see now that he had to get some cash together before he could go to New York and try to get into the theatrical world, but at that time it was a letdown.

That's when I got real mean. I don't think I've ever been so mean to anyone. He was just as nice as always until I made a nasty remark about how maybe he wasn't such a genius as he'd thought. Then he got mad at me. We had real words and it all ended up that I got talking of divorcing him, and then thinking about really doing it. In a way, this broke Albert's heart. He was very quiet after that, and said he'd never stand in the way of me doing anything I thought best for me."

Mrs. Watt sighed. "Well, I did divorce him. A girl friend of mine worked me up to it—girl friends do that. A couple of years later I married Watt. He was a pharmacist—a nice, steady job. I could give up my job at the plant. Now we own our own drugstore, out in Inglewood." Mrs. Watt sighed again.

"So the gist of what you came here to tell me is that in your opinion Albert was not the type of man apt to get murdered by his wife."

"Or anyone else," said Mrs. Watt, with a decided nod. "It just doesn't go with what I know of him. Of course, that was a long time ago, but people don't change so much. I haven't told you half the things I meant to, all things that show you how Albert was, all things that show how silly, how really *silly* it is to believe for a minute that *anyone* could hate Albert enough to murder him in cold blood."

The phrase "in cold blood" seemed to cheer Mrs. Watt. Some of her early excitement returned. *"Not* in cold blood," she repeated.

Tuck rose and thanked her for coming. She offered to sign anything he might want her to sign, and he explained that opinions are not quite the same as evidence, and that therefore he would not take her formal deposition. She looked disappointed.

"But what you have told me throws an interesting light on other information," he said to her gravely.

This pleased her. She drew on her very shiny black kid gloves with quite an air. Tuck stood for a moment in the doorway of the office watching her march importantly down the marble length of the outer corridor toward the elevators, back to Inglewood and George.

As he closed the door he reflected that what he had just told Mrs. Watt was quite true. Her rambling discourse had served to bring back to his mind the curious notion that had struck him while he circled the lake with Froody, that Albert Hime had been killed not because he was Albert Hime, but because he was Victoria Jason Hime's husband. That he had died as a pawn in a strange game in which Victoria, not knowing it, was the opponent to be destroyed. That within an unsound mind there was a hatred which had done this thing.

He thought again of what he knew of murder in passion. For a long time it had been waiting, this malignancy, and for some reason not known to him had flowered when it did. Had seen and had seized upon a means of causing Victoria pain—not death, but pain. Loss, grief, and perhaps at the last, after a long losing fight, conviction as a murderess.

The means had been so simple—a box containing ant poison, a silver bowl containing sugar. At long last, two simple objects conspiring with the capacity to torture hidden within a human skull.

He thought suddenly but not irrelevantly of the grinning tin masks which hung on Victoria's walls.

Within the thick yellowed walls of her house, Victoria was belatedly opening her birthday gifts which all during the preceding week had been arriving by mail, by messenger, and in the hands of the oldest and most intimate of her fifty intimate acquaintances. Earlier in the evening the telephone had rung frequently; everyone had been sympathetic and had shown as little curiosity as possible. Six notes of condolence had arrived in the morning mail. And a summons to the coroner's inquest, to be held on Tuesday morning at nine.

She was wearing her slacks again, and around her shoulders was a thick scarlet knitted shawl with gypsy fringe. The little red eye of the thermostat glared from the corner, but the house seemed cold. At her feet the crumpled white snow of tissue paper mounted; as she unwrapped each gift she set it down on the coffee table.

She surveyed the array. For the first time these gifts meant more to her than the sheer materialistic joy of new possession, or even the thoughtfulness which had prompted the giving. They were like a bulwark against a fear in her own mind. They were a reminder of the fact that people liked her, a good many people.

She still felt cold. She decided that something was wrong with the furnace, and went over and stood with her hands fanned out above the grating in the floor. No, it wasn't that. Quite a lot of warm air gushed up at her face. She decided to build a fire.

It was while she was squatting on the hearth, coaxing a match to ignite the twist of paper under the wood, that she heard it again. The sound outside.

She went quickly to the front door, hesitated a moment, then opened the top half abruptly and widely and peered out into the darkness. She listened. She heard only the thin shrill sound of the crickets in the orchard next door, the sound of traffic below on the boulevard.

She shut the door's upper half, and stood staring reflectively at the floor. Then she turned and went back to her gifts.

She had been hearing it all evening. It was always the same sound. Sometimes from the front of the house, sometimes from the narrow side yard to the north, sometimes from the back. As though someone, trying to move with utter silence, had inadvertently struck a stone with his foot and then had at once frozen to motionlessness.

She knew all the logical explanations for this phenomenon, the chief of which was a magnification by her own nerves of a perfectly normal sound, usually unnoticed.

She knew this, but it did not keep from her mind the mood which obsessed it, the conviction that the night around her house was not empty of an inhabitant, a watcher who hated her.

*Chapter Ten:*
## SUCH BEAUTIFUL HANDS

TUCK TELEPHONED Captain Harriss at nine the next morning. The man sounded sleepy and irritated. Tuck identified himself, said he wished to talk to Harriss at once, could be at his hotel in half an hour. "The Homicide Squad?" demanded Harriss, sharply. "What have I done in the last few days to get you interested in *me?*"

Tuck said he would explain that when he saw him.

It was one of those rare beautiful fall mornings. Tuck drove west out Sunset through white sunlight, under a clean blue sky.

Standing in the dark carpeted hotel corridor, he heard music coming from Captain Harriss's room, Mexican music, plaintively gay. Harriss opened the door abruptly after Tuck's knock. Harriss's shirt was open at the throat, exposing a triangle of hairy chest. In one hand was a bathroom glass which appeared to contain a mixture of whisky and water. His short dark hair was rumpled, his eyes were dark and reflectionless. Tuck's net impression was of virility and self-assurance, an impression aided by the heavy mustache which the man wore.

"Come in," said Harriss, abruptly. He nodded toward the room's one upholstered chair, himself straddled a straight chair facing it, resting the glass on the chair's back. "Care for a drink?" he asked, lifting the glass an inch in invitation.

"No, thanks," Tuck said. The room faced north, and was without sunlight. Outside the bright day shone.

The music he had heard was coming from the portable radio on the table beside the bed. Backed by the sound of guitars a woman's voice was singing. It was a strange voice, and for a moment it commanded Tuck's attention. It was a deep voice, almost hoarse, and there was fury and power in it. She was singing a Mexican *mariachi*, called *Cuatro Milpas*.

"She's dead," said Captain Harriss, gesturing toward the battered portable with his glass. The song ended; he got up and turned off the radio. "She died two days ago in Cuernavaca. Her name was Lucia Rio. She killed herself with sleeping pills. I once knew her quite well."

His opaque eyes looked into Tuck's. "What did you want to see me about?"

"On last Thursday evening you visited your ex-wife, Victoria Hime. Her husband died that same night in rather unusual circumstances. I came to see if you could throw any light on a few little matters."

Harriss's face did not change much. His brows raised by the fraction of an inch. "I never saw the guy," he said flatly.

Tuck nodded. "I know that."

"What did he die of?"

"Poison."

"Poison," repeated Harriss.

"Yes. According to what we've been able to learn, this poison was either administered accidentally by the servant who prepared the dinner which he ate shortly after returning home, or else he was murdered."

Harriss reflected. "There was no servant around when I was there," he said.

"No. The meal was prepared by her the evening before. Mrs. Hime then heated and served it."

"I see." Harriss rose, took a cigarette from the pack lying on the dresser near the whisky, lighted it, waved out the match, threw it into the wastebasket beside the dresser. "What does this have to do with me?" he asked.

"You were married to Mrs. Hime for a year, from 1934 to 1935," Tuck said.

"That's true, but scarcely relevant."

"What was your reason for visiting her last Thursday evening? I understand it had been ten years since you last saw each other."

"I visited her because I wanted to see her again. I was given a short leave before starting on my new assignment. I decided to spend it in Hollywood. I decided to look Victoria up while I was here."

"Nothing unusual occurred during your visit to her?"

"Nothing."

"You remained alone in the house while she went to fetch her husband whose car had broken down."

"That's right."

"Why?"

"I wanted to meet her husband."

"But you left before they returned."

"Right."

"Why?"

"I changed my mind about wanting to meet him."

"You left the house at about what time?"

"At about a quarter to eight. I'm not sure of the exact time."

"While you were there, did you enter the kitchen?"

"Yes."

"Did you happen to notice that one of the green canisters on the sideboard at right angles to the sink contained ant poison?"

"I did not."

"You saw the canisters?"

"I saw them, yes. They face you as you come in the door."

"You did not notice that the second one from the end, nearest the sink, had on its side a white label with a red edge on which had been lettered in ink the words *Ant Poison?*"

"No."

"Was there anything out of the ordinary about Mrs. Hime's attitude when you saw her?"

Captain Harriss stood up. He went to the radio again and turned it on, softly. After the tag end of an announcement in Spanish, another record began to play. It was the same woman singing.

"No, there was nothing out of the ordinary about Victoria," said Captain Harriss. He seemed almost to be smiling under the heavy mustache.

He added, "Taking into account the fact that she is, by and large, the most extraordinary woman I have ever known."

"Did she say anything to you about her husband?"

"Nothing except his name."

"Did she say anything to you about a young actress named Moira Hastings?"

Harriss cocked his head. "Nothing." He walked to the chair again, again straddled it. "Let me ask you one or two questions, just to get a few things straight in my mind. When was Hime poisoned? That is, when did he eat whatever contained the poison that killed him?"

"A short time before, or during, or after dinner."

"Ah," said Harriss. "Do you know what poison killed him?"

"Sodium fluoride."

At this Harriss reacted. His head went slowly and stiffly back. "So?" he said, softly. His eyes were alert now, more alive. "The ant powder."

Tuck said, "Not many people know that most ant poisons contain sodium fluoride as the basic ingredient, Captain Harriss."

Captain Harriss said, "Did you happen to read Victoria's book *Ina Hart?*"

Tuck nodded.

"So did I." After a pause, he asked, "Who is this Moira Hastings you mentioned?"

"A young actress. Mr. Hime was a film producer."

"Oh. A business associate, I see."

"Of course," said Tuck, "there's nothing tangible to disprove the fact that the man died as a result of carelessness on the part of the servant. Nothing, really, at all. She, of course, denies such an accident; that proves nothing. There seems to be no possible motive on anyone's part for murdering Mr. Hime. There is, however, the annoying matter of opportunity. Besides the servant, four people had the opportunity to use that poison in the kitchen. The actress, Miss Hastings, who had tea with Mrs. Hime. Her friend, Bernice Saxe—"

"Bernice," said Harriss. "Is she around? Good old Bernice."

"Yourself—"

Harriss laughed, his white teeth showing suddenly and ferociously under his mustache. "Hell's bells, man!" he said.

"And Mrs. Hime."

Sawn Harriss sobered abruptly. He went to the dresser, picked up the bottle, looked at it, put it down with a click. He turned, leaning against the dresser on his elbows, his feet crossed in front of him and supporting his weight. The voice of the singer was muted and passionate in the background. Harriss looked up at Tuck, his bold dark face brooding and quiet. He jerked his close-cropped head in the direction of the radio. "I read about her death in this morning's paper. A few lines. She was a great singer. She took dope, she drank too much, she had a cruel, ugly, primitive face, but when she sang she was great and you were great, listening to her. She always loved men who were not good to her. She always said that one day she would kill herself. All Latins threaten that. It's a form of self-expression with them. Whenever she told me that, three years ago in Mexico City, I laughed at her. I didn't believe it. I knew it was impossible."

He stood there silent for a moment, listening to the recording of the dead woman's voice. He spoke very quietly.

"Don't ask me whether I think Victoria could have killed her husband. I don't know."

After the door closed behind Tuck the singer's passionate voice grew louder. Harriss had turned up the radio as high as possible. Tuck left him listening to the voice of the woman who was dead.

At noon on Sunday Victoria was lying on the brilliant blue mat of the sun chair on the balcony, wearing a brief sunsuit of the same vivid blue. From the kitchen window above where she lay came the sound of Hazel humming as she ironed; from the living-room came the large noises of the New York Philharmonic concert. Victoria lay flat, her arms crossed on her forehead to make a cave of shadow for her eyes, thinking nothing, feeling nothing, only half hearing, only half-alive.

She scarcely heard the doorbell ring, nor Hazel answer it. The sound that made her lower her arms and open her eyes was the heavy sound of masculine footsteps on the floor of the dining-room, and then Sawn's voice speaking. "Hello, little friend."

He was standing in the open doorway, looking down at her. As she struggled to a sitting posture against the tilted back of the long chair he went solidly and with assurance to one of the canvas-seated white metal chairs huddled around the white table, scraped one into a position facing her, sat down.

He managed to look exceedingly comfortable sitting there, his hands on the arms of the chair, one leg cocked over the other. He continued to look at her, expressionlessly.

"You're wondering why I'm here," said Sawn, belatedly removing his cap and tossing it sideways to the table.

"I am." Victoria felt oddly defenseless in her brief shorts, her face bare of lipstick and shining with sun oil. Her voice, she realized, was unduly sharp.

"I want to talk about what happened to your husband."

"I don't," said Victoria to Sawn. She lay down again, once more shadowed her eyes with her arms.

"I never knew you to hide your head in the sand before," said Sawn. There was malice in his voice as he added, "You are usually so direct."

She didn't reply.

"All right, then I'll talk," said Sawn. She heard the snick of a match being lighted, smelled burning tobacco. "I haven't got a very clear picture yet, but the detective who questioned me this morning gave me some notion of what happened. And I'm mighty damned curious."

Victoria forced her eyes to remain closed, forced her voice to be very casual. "Oh. Mr. Tuck questioned you this morning?"

"Yes. I believe he came to find out whether, in my opinion, you could have poisoned your husband." He paused. "I told him I didn't know."

"That was white of you," said Victoria dryly.

"But since then I've done some thinking. I've done some wondering."

Victoria dropped her arms, swung herself to one elbow; on

her lips words were already forming which would tell Sawn that she had no intention of being questioned by him. But his blank, almost placid face, tipped a little forward and looking steadily toward her, made any such outcry seem childish, pettish. She swung her legs over the edge of the long chair, stood up, put on the white terry cloth robe lying across its foot.

"Is she pretty?" asked Sawn.

Victoria paused in the act of tying the robe's sash. "Who?"

"The actress. Moira Hastings."

"Very."

She sat in a chair across the table from him. The glare of sunlight on its white surface hurt her eyes; the metal arms of the chair were almost too hot to touch. Sawn's eyes seemed impervious to the glare, and his body to the heat. They were on hers with a ruthless and impersonal curiosity. "I'm trying to pin down what you once were and what you may be now," he said. "I find it hard. The years do queer things to people. What you have always wanted to be, and what you have become, is that rather fabulous creature, a self-sufficient woman, functioning like a man in a man's world." He rested one arm on the edge of the table, leaned over it a little toward her. "You always had to be first, Victoria. That's part of it. But there's another reason, I think, for your becoming that person. I wonder if you know about it. People know really so little about the lining of their minds. They have a fantastic ability to see of themselves little more than the picture they themselves create; the self that shows, the self the world sees. So I wonder if you yourself know the most important reason for your becoming such a very successful woman."

They stared at each other across the little table. "Your face," said Sawn.

The two words brought an old ache sharply back to Victoria. The ache that came when she ran into a hall of her childhood, heard her mother say to a woman over a teacup—the light voice behind the thick green plush portiere—"Victoria is not a pretty child, but she's a wonderfully intelligent one." And then the mirror of the mahogany hatrack, a faintly greenish oval, holding a sharp, pointed child's face with gray eyes. That was the first time that ache came to her.

"My face," she said, "has never been my fortune."

Sawn stood up, walked to the thick adobe wall with its row of potted cacti. He threw his cigarette over the wall, and she was reminded of seeing him make that same gesture on the night Albert had died. With his back to her he stood looking at the sprawled city under the wide blue sky.

"The last time we talked together you told me some interesting things about myself. Now I'm going to do the same for you. If you had been born pretty, your life would have been a very different one. I believe that you learned early that things that came easily to the pretty ones would not come to you. I believe you learned early that you were smart and talented, and that you would never be beautiful. You drove yourself forward with what you did have, brains and talent. Your face *has* been your fortune, Victoria."

He turned and faced her, looking down. "When I first knew you, I used to wonder at your friendship with Bernice. I used to wonder what you really felt when you saw her moving so easily through the large rooms of her husband's house, of which her pretty face had made her the mistress.

"On the memorable night of the blonde in the shower, I thought I knew the answer. You hated that girl. You hated her fully and hugely. You frightened her, you hated her so. It vibrated on the air. That's why she ran out: She was afraid of you. She was afraid of what you might do to her. I have always believed that if she had not been so pretty—so damnably, pink-and-white, pretty—you wouldn't have gone up in flames that night. You wouldn't, perhaps, have left me.

"It was not the conviction that I had been unfaithful that got you. It was that I had been unfaithful with beauty. It negated for you all you had achieved so far. It said to you that however hard you worked, you would never compensate for a basic lack you could do nothing about. That's what turned you crazy."

It was a strange moment. The warm sunlight, the wide blue sky, the little walled place in which they faced each other, the words just spoken.

"Believing this," said Sawn, "I find myself wondering. I find myself thinking of your husband and this actress. I find myself wondering what ten years may have done to you. I find myself wondering what such a betrayal would make you do now."

His eyes dropped to her two hands, holding tightly to the arms of her chair. "You have beautiful hands," he said. "I find myself thinking of those hands doing something swift and secret with poison. Scooping poison up in a spoon, stirring it into something your husband ate or drank. Your poor, damned, helpless hands obeying a hurt and an anger beyond your control for a little while."

There was nothing now on his face, not even curiosity. His skin was ruddy in the sunlight, his cheekbones prominent, like an Oriental's.

"As an amateur psychologist you do rather well," said Victoria. Her voice sounded thin.

"But then, of course," said Sawn, "I have to remember that I hate women. I have to remember that." He added, "They have two approaches: to possess or to abase themselves. Most of them really enjoy the last the best."

"That is as glib a generality as I have ever heard," said Victoria calmly.

"You would need to possess," said Sawn. "Did you possess Albert?"

Victoria looked at him steadily. "I am thinking of Greenwich Village in 1933. Crowded parties where everyone wrote or painted and where there were always a few Lesbians to remind us that we were the ultimate in sophistication. I am thinking of all the cheap, bright theories about life, coined and polished earlier in the day and brought forth in the evening and spent in order to gain a few minutes' attention from the crowd."

Sawn asked, "What was it that killed your husband? I mean, how was the poison administered?"

"It was in the sugar bowl," said Victoria, "which my servant filled the night before."

Below the dark mustache his mouth opened showing a gleam of white teeth and then closed again.

There was the soft scuffle of footsteps, and Hazel came through the open French door, a tray containing a plate of sandwiches and two tall glasses of iced coffee held stiffly level. She set the tray down on the table with a metallic sound. She looked at Victoria and said, "But I'm sure I didn't make any mistake and use the ant poison instead of the sugar. I've told Mr. Tuck that. I've sworn to it."

Then she turned and went away, her black kid slippers with their pompons making a sibilant sound.

Victoria stared after her. The calm finality of Hazel's statement, coming when it did, unnerved her slightly.

"Well," said Sawn. He added, "Well, well, well." Victoria looked at him, and was shocked. His whole face seemed to have come alive. Then he leaned forward toward her, and the reflection of the sun on the white table warmed his face, put sparkle into the dark irises of his eyes. "There is a dead woman named Lucia Rio," he said, "who killed herself with sleeping pills. At first her death puzzled me; but I think I know now how it happened. She had thought so often of doing that, that one night her hands did it by themselves. She was drunker than usual, I imagine, and one more man had hurt and angered her. It was late and she was alone and the tablets were there beside the bed, and the hands reached out for them and used them." He stood up. He walked to the door and turned to say, "Latins make so little of a little death, a little blood. I have to remind myself that it's quite different here."

Victoria knew that she would never forget his face, looking down at her.

*Chapter Eleven:*
## GRAY WARNING

THE CORONER'S inquest into the death of Albert Hime took place at one o'clock on the Tuesday following his death. It was held in a small tan-paneled courtroom in the Los Angeles City Hall. The inquest could have been delayed pending the uncovering of further evidence by the police, but Tuck, Gufferty, and the District Attorney were of the opinion that the nature of the case did not warrant such a delay. The District Attorney was sure that only a confession of guilt would conclusively solve it.

Tuck was fairly certain what the outcome of the inquest would be—a verdict of murder at the hands of a person or persons unknown, although this would depend to some extent on the coroner and on the coroner's jury also. He had seen coroner's juries whose personality ranged from lethargic stupidity which docilely went by the letter of the coroner's summing up of the evidence to juries who boldly brought forth an unexpected decision as to where guilt lay. So he could not be sure.

Victoria Hime, wearing a gray striped suit and a wide, tilted black felt hat, looked hard, capable, and determined. Tuck noted the strength and purity of the line of her jaw, the coolness of her clear gray eyes, the sternness of her wide mouth. She testified as to the identity of the deceased. She asserted her belief that he had not killed himself. She described briefly the last dinner they had eaten together.

The coroner, a precise man, gray of face and hair, showed some confusion over the matter of the sugar, for which Tuck could not blame him.

"The gist of it, then, Mrs. Hime, is that you used no sugar from the bowl on the table, whereas your husband did?"

"Yes."

"You yourself placed this bowl on the table?"

"Yes."

"When?"

"About an hour before we ate."

"Did you fill this bowl?"

"No."

"Who did?"

"My servant, Hazel Bennett."

Victoria concluded her testimony by covering the facts that she and her husband had rinsed the dishes, a customary procedure on Hazel's night off, had spent a pleasant, quiet evening, had retired early. She told of taking a sleeping pill, adding that the sound sleep it induced had kept her from hearing her husband call her, if he had called. She mentioned having heard her husband sending a telegram for a gift for her birthday.

"And when was your birthday?"

The wide mouth became tight and narrow. "The following day."

"The day you found him dead?"

"Yes." There was not the slightest change of expression, no tinge of self-pity on the woman's cool face. Glancing at the faces of the jury, Tuck saw the pity that Victoria Hime's face had not shown. He realized that her self-control had impressed them far more than tears would have done.

Hazel Bennett was called to the stand next. Although she had never before looked so, in the witness box she looked like a servant. After the smart severity of Victoria's clothes, Hazel's black, loose-hanging coat was dowdy, her straw hat with its white flower was hand-me-down, and her hands, clutching the strap of her bulging black purse, were the hands of the insecure.

She looked terribly frightened. Her voice came out with an effort, her pallid eyes blinked behind her glasses, she frequently had to pause before answering, and while she paused she wet her soft sagging lips with a furtive tongue. The faces of the jury watched her at first with a slightly condescending amusement which changed to interest as her testimony regarding the destruction of the poison came out reluctantly. After that matter had been made clear, the coroner's gray lips asked, crisply, "You filled the sugar bowl that was on the table on the night Mr. Hime died?"

"Yes, sir."

"When?"

Pause. "Well, it was the night before, I guess."

Sharply. "You guess?"

"It was the night before. After I'd washed the dinner things."

"Kindly describe for the jury the arrangement of the cans in which you kept the sugar and so forth."

Hazel described them.

"In other words, they were identical except for the lettering on the front of each can denoting its contents?"

"Yes."

"How big were these letters?"

"About a half—no, about three-quarters of an inch high."

The coroner held up a card. This card was green and on it was printed in letters about an inch high SUGAR.

"What does that say?"

Hazel hesitated. She squinted. She leaned a little forward, peering intently through the thick lenses of the rimless glasses which sharpened her world to visibility. "Sugar!" she announced, triumphantly.

The coroner arranged the card precisely on his desk and then turned to the jury. "It has seemed important to establish for you the fact that this woman is extremely nearsighted. I chose to do so in as graphic a way as I could think of."

He turned to Hazel and said pleasantly, "Now, Mrs. Bennett, was it possible that in your hurry to get home on Wednesday evening you might have—*might* have, I say—reached for the can which contained the ant poison rather than the can which contained the sugar?"

"No, sir! No such thing happened."

Hazel was excused. Fear was on her face as she took her place among the other witnesses in the first and second rows of seats.

If Hazel's testimony had weighed in Victoria's favor, Bernice's hat did so to even greater extent. Tuck decided, looking at it with unprejudiced eyes, that it was the most extravagantly ridiculous hat he had ever seen. Although dressed entirely in severe black, Bernice had allowed herself one flourish. The hat which topped her sleek coiffure was made entirely of pink feathers, overlapping like the feathers of a bird. The hat dipped crazily down over one wide brown eye, and what held it to her head he could not guess. From the exact center of the round forward-tilted pink-feathered crown, which was about the circumference of a pancake, a startled-looking fluff of black leaped toward the eye of the beholder. That hat made Bernice look like a foolish, giddy woman, quite capable, for a foolish, giddy reason, of getting rid of the poison in her friend's kitchen.

Bernice's breathless, tiny voice went with the hat. "—so I just thought, why not throw it away, then everything will be all right?" (Shiny, girlish brown eyes raised to the impassive face of the coroner.) "I mean, it was a dreadful thing to do, I realize that, but I was *so* upset!"

The look on the face of the coroner was echoed on the faces of the five men in the jury box. It was a look of conscious masculine superiority. The women were looking at the hat.

Bernice was excused, with a sharp comment from the coroner on her witless destruction of evidence. She took this meekly, her lids lowered over her eyes.

To establish the impossibility of the administration of the poison before dinnertime, George Leighman and Moira Hastings testified.

Leighman's brief evidence proved that Albert had partaken of nothing but black coffee during their chat in the café before dinner. Under questioning from the coroner he elaborated on his relationship to the dead man and his wife. When he spoke of Victoria, his voice was warm with admiration and friendliness.

Moira Hastings provided the highlight of the day, and the only surprise for Tuck. She was also in black, with a little white jeweled collar. Her eyes were jewels too, and looked too heavily made up in the revealing light. Her voice was soft and clear—the voice of a lady. She did not cross her legs. Her hat was as noticeable as Bernice's had been, but in a happier way. It was a little round tipped box covered with small gleaming stones like those sewed to her collar.

She confirmed Mr. Leighman's testimony, explained that Mr. Hime had eaten or drunk nothing after Leighman and her agent had departed.

Clearing his throat, the coroner spoke. "During a conversation with the detective investigating this case, you made the statement that Mrs. Hime was jealous of you. You stated as your reason the fact that she did not want you to have the leading role in her husband's forthcoming picture. Will you please reiterate this opinion for the jury." He turned to the jury. "Opinions are not evidence, of course."

And then Tuck got his jolt. "I may have somehow given Mr. Tuck that impression," she said. "I don't remember what I said. But if I did give such an impression, I am terribly, terribly sorry for it, because it would be terribly, terribly wrong.

At the time I was questioned about this awful thing, I had just learned of Mr. Hime's death. It was a terrible shock to me. He had been most kind to me during our business discussions, and had given me much encouragement, a thing a young actress often needs. I was so upset over his death that I wouldn't be surprised at anything I may have said. But I have only the greatest respect and admiration for Mrs. Hime. I consider her to be a brilliant and unusual woman."

In his instructions to the jury, the coroner pointed out that the burden of proof against any one person rested entirely with the state, that unless such proof had been offered the jury could not find any person responsible, accidentally or otherwise, for the death of Albert Hime. He pointed out that murder because of negligence was still murder, although to a lesser degree. He pointed out that the poison which had been in the kitchen had actually been available to anyone who saw it and who might have conceived, for an unknown reason, the notion of putting some of it into the sugar bowl. He explained that the conclusions of a coroner's jury do not end a case of criminal investigation; and that if on the strength of present evidence, they were unable to fix the matter of guilt, if they should find that Mr. Hime had met death at hands other than his own, the police would continue to investigate the problem until enough evidence against some person might be revealed. This person could be then arrested for his crime and brought to trial. In short, all the jury had to determine, to the best of their ability, was whether Mr. Hime had been murdered. If they found he had, then they could, if they wished, recommend that any certain person or persons be held as having been responsible for his death. They did not have to do so, but could do so if they felt the evidence against any one person merited it.

The coroner's jury was out for an hour. They returned with a verdict of murder at the hands of a person or persons unknown. As the courtroom was cleared, Tuck watched the jurymen depart. Six pairs of eyes strayed to the face of Hazel Bennett, six to that of Victoria Jason Hime.

Victoria Hime left the courtroom between George Leighman's hovering bulk and Bernice Saxe's pink hat. Tuck found himself just behind them as they all waited for the elevator. He heard Victoria say, "It was really anticlimactic. Just the facts pulled out one by one, and looked at by that faintly interested jury."

Tuck said, "That's all it could be, you see. Just the facts we have to date."

Tuck saw Moira Hastings waiting a little apart from the others. He watched her attentively. She met his gaze coolly. She apparently assumed that a member of the police force would not be shocked at what might seem like perjury—which was true. Tuck was not at all shocked. He was very, very interested.

George Leighman nodded and smiled perfunctorily at Moira Hastings. Tuck became a little less interested in her. The reason why she had changed her testimony was now apparent to him.

The small hard knot of fear which had been inside her chest for three hours was still there when Victoria stepped into the elevator. She wondered that it had not vanished with the jury's verdict.

"Well," said Bernice in her ear, "that's over!"

After the inquest Victoria went to the mortuary at the foot of her own street. Bernice went with her. Albert looked so un-dead in his casket that it was a little horrible. The two women stood looking down at him.

They said nothing until they were in Walter's large closed car with its gray plush seats. Then Bernice said, "I wonder, would you mind going with me while I shop for the baby's layette?"

"Isn't it a little premature?" asked Victoria.

They went to several of the big stores on Wilshire; Bernice cooed softly over ruffly pink bonnets, tiny shirts and gowns. "I *love* babies," she said.

All through the orgy of soft pinks and blues, of fluffy blan-kets, of cribs with ducks and bunnies, Victoria thought of Al-bert in his casket. Bernice bought a woolly white lamb which she carried home with her. Victoria held it on her lap in the car; she was to have dinner with Bernice and Walter.

Dinner was served by candlelight in the large dining-room. Walter sat at the head of the table, Bernice at the foot, Victoria halfway between them. Mrs. Buxton served an excellent meal in utter silence.

Bernice looked lovely. She had on a soft blue dinner gown. There was something changed in the relationship between Walter and Bernice, Victoria saw at once.

Over dessert Walter waxed a little loquacious. "Well, it's

been a bad time for you, Victoria," he said, "but you'll weather it."

He added, slowly turning the stem of his wineglass, "You career women interest me; you have a sound practicality, an ability to take care of yourself which I must say I admire. Most women are, to some degree, parasites. Not their fault, of course. Legally, they were regarded as chattels in the most civilized countries of the world until very recently." His gaze fell for a moment on Bernice, returned to Victoria. Victoria wondered for the first time if there was a streak of cruelty in Walter.

"I found the loveliest white lamb today, Walter," said Bernice, from the foot of the table.

His eyes went to her fondly and tolerantly. "Did you, my dear? And what did it cost, this wonderful lamb?"

Bernice said, "Eighteen dollars. It's *so* sweet!"

Walter looked at Victoria. "Would *you* pay eighteen dollars for a white lamb?" he asked, humorously.

"I have no particular fondness for lambs," said Victoria.

"I don't think you would," said Walter, still smiling. "But then you earn the money you spend."

She waited for a decent moment before she looked at Bernice. If Bernice had felt the sting in the words, she didn't show it. She was looking at Walter still with that gentle submissiveness.

The next afternoon when Victoria went out to the mailbox on the left of the adobe gateposts flanking the mouth of the driveway there was only one letter. It was for her. She noticed with idle interest that the name and address had been printed in capitals. The two lines on the heavy gray paper inside were also printed: IT IS NOT OVER YET. YOU ARE GOING TO SUFFER NOW.

She stared down at the page in her hands. The sunlight twinkled on her platinum wedding band. A bird sang. From somewhere up the street a dog barked.

Victoria put the note carefully back into its envelope. She saw from the postmark that it had been mailed late the evening before. Her mind admitted what she had not before admitted to herself. That she had never quite believed in the accident on Hazel's part. That almost from the moment she had looked down and seen Albert lying dead, there had been a haunting sense of an evil behind his dying. This vague, half-knowledge had been repressed, held back, and it now burst forth with double force for the withholding.

*The ability to destroy*—the words were framing neatly and carefully in her mind as though she were speaking them aloud—*is as latent in the human soul as the ability to create. To destroy may become a necessity, under certain inner pressures. It doesn't mean insanity, although that's the simplest word for it.*

*Chapter Twelve:*
## TUCK PLAYS A TRUMP

SHE LATER regarded it as strange that Sawn's face, the older face which had replaced the thinner, young one, should have been sharp in her mind when the old gardener called to her. "Mrs. Hime!"

She turned and saw him just the other side of the fence, stooping a little to peer below the intervening black branch of one of the trees before her house. This time he had his hand curled around a rake rather than a spade, but otherwise his appearance was the same as on the morning after Albert's death when he had so startled her by peering into Albert's room. The old felt hat, dingy with sweat, the faded blue shirt rolled back at the cuffs, the sagging vest, the sagging trousers, and the faded old blue eyes.

"Hello!" she answered. He stepped carefully over the low picket fence, eased himself to her yard with a long step, and came toward her, his feet scuffling through the ivy below the trees with a snakelike sound. "I been thinking I should tell you something," he said, as he reached her. "About that fellow who come to see you Sunday about noon. The big fellow in the uniform."

"Yes?" asked Victoria. "Yes, Mr. Livingstone?"

"He was the one," said Mr. Livingstone, nodding. "He was the one all right. I could tell from the uniform, and the way he walked, kind of cocky. It was moonlight that night, bright moonlight."

"I wish I knew what you meant," said Victoria.

"Oh. Well, he did something kind of funny, the night your husband died. I live out back over the garage, you know about that. It was close on to three o'clock, and most of the party was over, and I was at my window opening it again, and I saw him. He come out of the side door of the house, lighting a cigarette. Then he walked straight over to the fence between the lots, and he stood there, looking at your house. He'd puff on his cigarette, blow out smoke and look. I wondered what he was looking at. That's how I come to be standing there that morning when you shut the curtains at me. I was wondering what he'd been looking at."

Why was it so strange to know that Sawn had been in the house next door, that it had been he, almost certainly, who had played those old half-forgotten songs on the piano? Why was it disturbing to know that he had indulged in that late vigil outside Albert's window?

She remembered the uneasiness of her lonely Saturday evening; the repeated feeling that someone was outside her house in the darkness. There had been, on one night at least, a watcher after all.

"Thank you for telling me this," she said.

"Always liked you," said Mr. Livingstone as he turned away. "Always liked a worker. Hear that typewriter of yours clickety-clacking while I work around the yard. Haven't heard it lately. Read in the paper about your husband dying. Sorry about that." He half turned as though to go, stopped to say reflectively, "It was queer, that fellow, to be staring so. Like he knew about it, only he couldn't have."

"No," said Victoria, "he couldn't have."

"Because," said Mr. Livingstone, "when he turned away I saw him clear in that moonlight, and he was smiling."

And Mr. Livingstone scuffed away through the dark green ivy, his feet making the sound of snakes, the fan-shaped bamboo rake cocked over one shoulder.

Victoria looked down at the envelope in her hand. She recalled another envelope, much smaller. A tiny white one, with a card inside: *Happy birthday, Victoria. Sawn.*

It was while she was waiting for Tuck to arrive that Albert's birthday gift came. She had half-forgotten that he had ordered something for her that last night of his life, and the small, much-stamped airmail package was at first a surprise, although she realized almost immediately what it must be. Hazel, who had opened the door and had received the package, hovered close while Victoria tore off the twine, the wrappings. Inside was a white box, and inside that, wedged with tightly stuffed tissue, was a jeweler's box. A small, humpbacked one of black velvet. She pressed the catch with her thumb and the lid sprang up. Inside was the most beautiful ring she had ever seen. A sapphire, her birthstone, square-cut and of a deep, deep blue. It was set in platinum, and on either side glittered a clump of small perfect diamonds. A tiny card was bent into the rounded lid of the box. It said, not in his handwriting, *Love, Albert.* The jeweler's name was in gold on the white satin of the lid. The ring had come from Tiffany's, from New York.

She slipped the slim band on the finger where her wedding ring shone. It fitted perfectly.

"Oh!" gasped Hazel. "Oh, my, what a beautiful thing!"

She heard Albert's dead voice speaking in the hall.

"Send to Mrs. Hime, above address." She turned her hand. The ring gleamed and glittered. "He always said I had beautiful hands," Victoria said, in a tight voice.

It was Hazel who began to cry. She fled to the kitchen as the doorbell rang. Victoria admitted Mr. Tuck. The impact of the gem which felt so strangely heavy on her hand was still with her. Tuck asked courteously, "What has happened, Mrs. Hime?"

Victoria held out her hand to him. He took the tips of her cold slim fingers in his long warm ones, bent his long head to peer at the ring. "Albert wired for this, for me, for my birthday. It just came. Isn't it lovely?"

Tuck nodded his head. "It's very beautiful," he said.

And then it poured out—Sawn's serenade, hearing Albert sending the telegram, Sawn's brief vigil in the early morning; a strange conglomerate of unrelated facts.

Then she showed him the anonymous note.

"You think Harriss sent this?" Tuck asked.

"I don't know! But I do know this: he is going to come to

you and tell you he thinks I killed Albert. He's going to tell you why he thinks so, specious reasons, which may sound true to you! I'm sure of that much, at least!"

Tuck looked down at the square envelope in his hands, stuffed it carefully into the inner pocket of his coat. "I think this was written by a woman," he said.

Victoria heard, yet did not hear. She said, "I'm afraid, Mr. Tuck. For the first time in my life, I'm afraid." Saying the words eased her.

"Of Captain Harriss?"

"Yes. Of him, or—of someone." Under his probing grave eyes she turned sharply away. "I sound like a fool." Then she faced him, holding out the hand with the ring. "Whatever anyone says to you, does it look as though Albert and I hated each other? Does it look as though we quarreled?"

Hazel's voice called, "Mr. Tuck!" She was standing in the kitchen doorway, a white dish towel in her hands. With her head high, she said, "I *could* have made that mistake with the poison, Mr. Tuck. If it's that or Victoria killing him, then I did!"

Tuck looked at her long and curiously, and at the ring, and at Victoria's tense face. Then he smiled almost sadly. "You two women do me an injustice," he said, slowly and carefully. "I make guesses. I have intuitions. I am not a strictly logical man."

His long and tired brown eyes were on Victoria's when he added, "Logic tells me nothing; a guess tells me that Hazel didn't accidentally poison the sugar; an intuition, a feeling which is very bothersome tells me that you are right in being afraid, Mrs. Hime."

He had left the house and was standing on the porch as he added, "I believe I may be getting ulcers of the stomach."

An hour later a mechanic returned Albert's car from the garage which had picked it up. Only after he had gone did she realize she had allowed him to leave it in the driveway where it would prevent her driving her own car to the street. Of course, there was no reason why she should not use Albert's; it was much handsomer than hers, which was of a popular make. But Albert's long black phaeton used a great deal more gasoline and was hard to park. So she backed Albert's car out to the street, parked it, drove hers out and parked it, and then drove Albert's into the depths of the deep but narrow garage. As she snapped off the ignition she realized that she had never before driven Albert's car; it seemed strange to be doing so now after he was dead. It seemed almost an intrusion.

She opened the glove compartment to see whether he might have left in it anything of importance, but found only a map, a pair of shabby pigskin gloves and a magazine. After she had returned her car to the garage she went up the steps of the house looking at the magazine. It was the *New Yorker*, the last issue but one. It was opened halfway through; the first thing her eyes fell on was a Tiffany ad. With a start, she recognized her ring. *Flanked by eight flawless diamonds, this perfect two-carat sapphire of deepest blue is without peer among gems. $1,985— Price includes 20% federal tax.*

The price dismayed her; she had not imagined, somehow, that sapphires were so costly. Then came a surge of pleasure, not because her ring had turned out to be such a valuable one, but because something she had always guessed of Albert had been confirmed. This brought him somehow close to her. Under the lack of ostentation which he imposed on himself, there had been a boyish enthusiasm for the lavish things, for making big gestures. All that he had told her of the poverty of his youth in Chicago explained that tendency; that he usually masked it was a part of the self-discipline which had gone to make him a successful man. This had shown itself in the enormous boxes of chocolates he brought so often, in his choice of big colorful bouquets of flowers. And now it had shown itself once again.

She saw now the pattern that underlay that late telegram. Albert had seen this ad she was looking at, he had thought of the ring on her hand. Later, reminded of her almost-forgotten birthday, he had ordered it, although it had cost a great deal, more than another man might have felt he could afford for a wife who would have been well content with much less.

Grief for Albert took charge of her heart.

She was not allowed this luxury for long. Bernice came.

Bernice was upset again, although next to the frightful panic which had gripped her during that other visit she could be considered calm, except that now, as then she forgot the usual gesture of removing her gloves. "It's Stan!" she burst out, as she flung herself onto the sofa. Her posture was unlike the slack, ungraceful pose of which she had been unconscious that other time. She sat like a woman on stage, remembering how to arrange her feet. "He's being a nuisance! He keeps calling!"

"Don't go to the phone," said Victoria, taking a cigarette from the box on the coffee table. Bernice took one too, and lighted it.

"I don't. I always have Mrs. Buxton say I'm not in but he keeps on calling. So far it hasn't happened while Walter's been home, but if it does it'll just be a red rag to a bull, and everything's been going so nicely!"

"Stan's taking it harder than I thought he would," said Victoria candidly.

"Oh, it's nothing but his sense of drama!" snapped Bernice. "He has to milk the situation of every drop of farewell stuff!"

Bernice stabbed out her cigarette. She looked at Victoria with large brown eyes. "Why don't *you* phone Stan and talk with him?" she asked suddenly. "I mean he knows you know all about everything. Remember that Richards boy I wanted to marry and that Mama hated so and how we'd go to movies and you'd let Mama think I'd gone with you?" Bernice's voice was bright, pressing this memory from the past to emphasize their long friendship, to coax Victoria into serving this present need.

"It's a ridiculous notion," said Victoria.

Bernice gave her a hard little glance. "Oh, all right I'll do it myself then."

Quite deliberately, Victoria listened to Bernice speaking in the little hallway. "Stan. This is Bernice. Stan you *must* stop calling me. . . . I mean it. . . . We *said* good-by. That's not true; you enjoy this sort of thing. Well, I don't. . . . Are you doing it out of malice? I've explained the whole thing to you." (Long pause.) "You never cared for anyone but yourself, Stan, but I'm asking you to stop phoning my house. What? Oh, is that so? Is *that* so? How about what you call your house; it belongs to your mother unless I'm much mistaken! . . . What? I'll be delighted to. I intended to do so anyhow but it was such a trifling little gift that I felt it might seem insulting. A messenger will deliver it to you tomorrow!"

Bernice returned shaken. "What a cheap little devil he is," she said, and sighed. She sat down wearily and her eyes misted with something like tears. "He wants his bracelet back; it seems it's really his mother's."

"That practically symbolic. So is he."

Bernice's roving and abstracted eye fell on Victoria's sapphire ring. She shot forward toward Victoria, one arm propping her weight. With the other hand she pointed. Her black-gloved finger was long and thin. "Where did you get that!"

Victoria told her.

Bernice, who was holding Victoria's ring hand in her own, suddenly flung it aside like something she was casting away. "It's ridiculous!" she said, contemptuously. "Why, he didn't make a quarter of what you do! It's in very bad taste, considering that! *Very* bad taste!"

"I thought it one of the kindest things anyone has ever done for me," said Victoria quietly.

Bernice flung her arms around Victoria, kissed the side of her face with lips that would leave, Victoria knew, a double red stain, like a bite.

"I'm mean!" she cried. "I'm venomous and selfish! How could I have said such a thing! It was sweet of him! It was dear of him!"

In her new agitation Bernice stood up, pacing restlessly before the coffee table on her tiny high-heeled feet. "I'm a terrible woman, terrible!" she cried. Her black-gloved hands went to her face and covered it. She stood there, her shoulders crouched in what seemed like shame, her face hidden in those cupped black hands. Muffled by the gloves came the whispered words, "When I think of what I let myself do because of that awful man—"

Suddenly she threw back her head, her face wary. "I'm not apologizing. Walter's no angel to live with. Walter has his little claws sometimes."

Then a wry, bitter smile touched her lips and she looked old. "Isn't it funny, how it goes with us?" she asked in her little-girl voice. "Whenever I'm in luck, you're out of it; whenever you're lucky, something awful's happening to me. Like two sides of a balance. It's always been that way." She added, dreamily, "I haven't been lucky for such a long, long time—"

Twenty-four hours after Tuck put the anonymous note into his inner coat pocket, Froody said to him, "Oh, there's no doubt about it. And it was an easy little job at that. There was the watermark on the stationery. And the fact it had been cut off to get rid of a name or initials at the top. I made the rounds of the Hollywood stationers. I went over the old order lists at the places carrying that brand of writing paper. At the fifth place I found her name on their list; she'd ordered two boxes six months ago."

"And the pen it was printed with?"

"The enlargements show one of the better pens—even ink flow, no scratching."

From the street below, traffic sounds wafted up. Tuck sat for a moment listening to them, and then went to the hatrack for his brown fedora.

"You going to talk to her?"

"Yes."

"Want me along?"

"No."

Froody looked wistful. "What I can't figure is why she did it. If she was out to get Mrs. Hime, she had her chance at the inquest, and she knocked herself out covering up for her. I don't get it." He brooded for a moment, and Tuck put on his hat. "'You're going to suffer now,'" quoted Froody. "That's queer. That's—wrong, somehow."

Moira Hastings was not at home, so Tuck waited for her in his shabby black sedan, which looked even shabbier than usual in comparison to the suave opalescent convertible coupé parked just ahead of him. The midafternoon sunlight, which always seemed clearer and brighter in Hollywood than in Los Angeles, beamed down on the chateau-like white building where Moira Hastings lived. A woman in slacks above which showed a brown diaphragm stared insolently at his car, went lightly up the steps of the apartment building. In half an hour Moira Hastings drove past without seeing him, and parked two spaces ahead up the sloping street. He was waiting for her at the door when she came up the steps, her key in her hand. Above a tailored beige jacket her amber hair shone brightly. Her hard light eyes flashed a hint of fear, and then she half-dropped her lashes and looked very noncommittal.

"I want to talk to you," he said. He took her elbow, turned her around, led her to his car.

"What do you want to talk about?" she asked, when he had tucked his bulk in under the steering wheel.

"The anonymous note you sent to Mrs. Hime."

She held her breath for a moment. "I don't know what you mean."

Tuck sighed, and turned on the ignition. He pressed his foot on the starter and the motor whirred.

Her voice was thin. "Where are you taking me?"

"To the city jail."

Her body went rigid, and the brown purse on her lap slid to the floor with a muffled thud. Tuck dropped one long arm and retrieved it, but instead of returning it he opened it and felt among the contents. She tried to snatch it from him, but he twisted his body and fended off her hands with one elbow. He took out her fountain pen and put it into his inner pocket. Politely, he laid the purse on Moira Hastings's lap.

"You can't do that!" she said.

"I've done it. The paper has been traced to you through the stationer where you had it printed with your name and address. Printing from this pen, enlarged, will match the printing of that note. I don't think it wise of you to continue to deny that you wrote and sent that note, but that's your business."

He slipped into low gear, stepped on the gas; the car moved forward.

"Wait!" Her fingers clamped tight on his forearm.

He had been so sure of what she would do that he had really taken his foot from the gas before she spoke. The car coughed and settled back into immobility. There was a silence.

"You couldn't have me jailed," said Moira Hastings. Her voice was unsteady.

Tuck nodded his head twice. "Oh, yes. On suspicion of murder. It's often done. It's an excellent way of holding a witness."

She tried to read his face. She settled back into the corner of the seat. "All right," she said. "I believe you."

"Then you'll talk."

She straightened. "This is dreadfully banal! They only say 'Then you'll talk,' in cheap gangster movies."

Tuck waited.

Moira Hastings moved her shoulders uneasily against the worn plush of the seat. "What do you want me to say? That I sent the note? All right, I sent it!"

In sepulchral tones Tuck quoted, "'It is not over yet. You are going to suffer now.'"

"Well, all right! I sent it! What more do you want me to say?"

"For the moment, nothing. I want you to listen. I want you to think. I mean think, and not let your emotions deceive you into the belief that you're doing so. I'm going to show you what that foolish note of yours told me about you. I hope I'm going to convince you that it would be hopeless for you to deny the truth about why you sent it. This will take a little time.

"To begin with, what does that note mean? It means this: 'You killed your husband, Mrs. Hime. So far you've got away with it, but you're not going to escape entirely. If nothing else, there's your own knowledge of what you've done, and you will live with that for the rest of your life.' That's all, absolutely all, that note could possibly be construed to mean. I think Mrs. Hime herself toys with the notion that there is some furtive menace in the words. But the writing of an accusing, unsigned note is the opposite of menacing. For one thing, the writer has, for some reason, to hide his identity, which means that he is to some extent impotent and knows it. For another—well, I'm reminded of the old childhood saying, 'Sticks and stones may break my bones, but names will never hurt me.' That note was a name-calling, really. Pretty weak stuff.

"The ambiguity of the note interested me. It implies a knowledge which you believed Mrs. Hime shared. What could that knowledge be? That she had killed her husband. Now if she had, that note would be a frightening thing to receive, because it showed that someone else knew what she had done. That is what you intended. You hoped to frighten her so that if she were guilty, perhaps at the end of her rope, she might, she just possibly *might* give herself up. This would accomplish an end you desired without wishing to give the information which would bring it about.

"It was a pretty thin hope, and ties in with the strongly dramatic flavor of the note, written by a person whose lack of experience with life enables her still to believe in the myth of the human conscience, to believe that a person capable of murder is capable of anguish over its commission. That is not usually the case.

"Now before you insult me by telling me that you were ter-

ribly, terribly shocked at the inquest into the death of a man
who had always been terribly, terribly kind to you, I'm going
to tell you why you were able to believe that Mrs. Hime killed
her husband.

"At first you said she was jealous of you. You gave as your
reason the fact that she had refused you a part you felt you
could handle. You also threw in gratis the suggestion of a psy-
chotic jealousy of all beautiful women. You are, by the way,
beautiful, Miss Hastings. I concede that.

"Now none of that bothered me. It didn't influence me either for or against Mrs. Hime. You see, the thought occurred
to me that one cannot attribute to others motives of which
he is not himself capable. A person too large to feel jealousy
doesn't recognize it in others. And the curious notion occurred
to me that you are extremely jealous of Mrs. Hime. That shows
a lot of greed when you have both youth and beauty, but you
want success. She has it. However, that is a little beside the
point.

"At the inquest you went back on your previous statement
as to Mrs. Hime's jealousy.

"At first this was rather a shock, I admit. But then the apparent reason became clear to me. There was Mr. Leighman,
who thinks so well of Mrs. Hime. You felt that to speak against
her in front of him would make him dislike you, and so make
him refuse to give you the part of Ina Hart. So, I told myself,
you had come to realize the untruth of that previous emotional
statement as to Mrs. Hime's jealousy of you. You were willing
to leave it behind under pressure of a new emotion, the hope

of getting the part after all, through Leighman, the executive producer.

"And then came that anonymous note. I saw I had been wrong. I saw another pattern behind those three actions—the first statement of Mrs. Hime's jealousy of you, the second act of retracting it at the inquest, the third act of writing the note.

"Here's where your agent comes in. He made it plain to you that involvement in a scandal would end your career. Hollywood is no longer a place of ermine toilet-seat covers and flagrant sin. Mrs. Hime belongs to a hard-working, intelligent group of people, the brains behind the camera, of which Mr. Leighman is one. Your agent knew or guessed what your first insistence on Mrs. Hime's jealousy should have suggested to me—that you and Albert Hime had for some months been lovers."

"That—is—not—true!" stated Moira Hastings, slowly and emphatically.

Tuck went on: "So you changed your tune at the inquest to clear yourself. Your agent showed you what such a statement as you made to me would suggest; you took his advice. But after the inquest you were boiling with rage against Mrs. Hime. It maddened you that she was going to escape punishment. It was additionally maddening to realize that you had been forced, you felt, to remain silent. You wrote the note."

"There was never anything like that between us!" cried Moira Hastings.

"You wrote the note and in doing so told me what I now know, that you had a very good reason to believe that Mrs.

Hime killed her husband. You believed that she discovered the
relationship between the two of you, went off balance with the
knowledge, and poisoned him."

Moira Hastings's eyes had an oddly blank look. He could
see that she was taking his earlier advice and thinking; thinking hard.

Watching her, he saw below the delicate skin of her throat
the hard gorge rise and tighten. Her hands were claws grasping the edge of her purse. Under the painted face he saw the
real one show through, a small, hard face of bone and mus-
cle. A nerve at the corner of her right eye twitched. The eye
continued to look forward at the windshield while the nerve
twitched a second time, and relaxed. For the first time he felt
her as a human being. He saw her as she had once been, a
hard-thighed little girl with sausage curls who had worn a bal-
let dress and had danced on her toes to the tinkle of a piano in
a roomful of other such children. An adoring mother had sat
by the wall watching and holding a sweater which would be
slipped about the bony, little-girl shoulders.

She turned suddenly toward him. "You've been right and
wrong," she said. Her voice was stripped of its usual color and
warmth; it was the voice of a mathematician stating an irrefut-
able equation. "It was only emotion that made me say she was
jealous of me. I thought so because she was against my getting
that part. My agent talked me out of that feeling. At the inquest I was thinking of my chances with Leighman. I never
had any intention of repeating all that stuff I said to you at the
first. When I saw Leighman there I laid it on with a trowel

and said what a swell gal she was. I had my career to think of. It might have swung the balance.

"And then, after I went home, something occurred to me in a new light. I wrote the note because I was sure she'd killed him. I wrote it hating her. He had been kind to me. I suddenly put two and two together and realized the servant couldn't have poisoned the sugar.

"She couldn't have. On Thursday afternoon, while Mrs. Hime was on the telephone, I drank a last cup of tea. Because I really like it best that way, I put sugar in it. Two spoonfuls. From the silver sugar bowl that was on the coffee table. The silver sugar bowl the servant filled."

They looked at each other.

Moira Hastings pressed down on the latch of the car door. It swung out into the bright sunlight. "As you can see, I'm not dead. I'm still around. There was no poison in that sugar at five o'clock. Play around with that for a while."

His voice stopped her. "Wouldn't it have been simpler to come to me with that information?"

The expression on Moira Hastings's face altered. The hard little-girl face vanished. Her eyes were wide as she said, "I thought I'd wait a while. I mean, I couldn't see any reason *why* she would have killed him, and you feel squeamish about putting someone's neck into a noose. I decided the note might make her tell, if she really did it. I'm sorry if that seems childish. I *have* always believed that a person who kills suffers pangs of remorse. Like Macbeth, you know. And like Lady Macbeth, washing her hands."

After Moira Hastings had gone, Tuck drew from his coat pocket a small notebook covered in black leather. He studied the close scrawl it contained, abbreviations so condensed that they constituted a sort of shorthand. He came to *coff c o sk aft Har wnt.* Then he returned the book to his pocket and drove to the nearest drugstore. Wedging himself into a telephone booth he called the Hollywood Roosevelt Hotel. Captain Harriss was in his room.

"You drank a cup of coffee while Mrs. Hime was out of the house on Thursday night," Tuck stated.

There was a short pause. "Yes."

"Do you use sugar in your coffee, Captain Harriss?"

"Yes."

"And you did so then?"

"Yes."

"And the sugar you used came from the silver bowl on the dinner table?"

There was a longer pause.

"Yes," said Captain Harriss.

"I'll want a deposition to that effect."

"Make it snappy."

There was a short silence. Then Harriss hung up so quietly that only the changed hum on the receiver told Tuck he had broken the connection.

*Chapter Thirteen:*
HOW IT WAS

VICTORIA HAD just brought Haggis home from the vet's when Tuck arrived. It was dusk. He bulked huge in her half-doorway. Haggis barked loudly at him, working herself into a frenzy at his feet, but he did not seem to notice her. "Tonight," he said to Victoria, "you are going to have visitors. I'll be one of them. I may be a little late in arriving, but I'll get here."

She said, "What visitors?"

"Miss Hastings. Mrs. Saxe. Captain Harriss." She noticed that his voice was crisper than usual. His eyes were different too.

"And what will you do?" she asked. "Will you stride up and down before us and say, 'I have known all along, of course, that one and only one person could have committed this murder. I am now going to show which of you did it, and why'?"

"Possibly," said Tuck. "I will also have a warrant of arrest in my pocket."

Victoria's heart pounded once, hard. "Isn't this all a little dramatic?" she asked.

"It's a short cut," said Tuck. He added, with a return of his old slowness, "It just may not work. It may be a fizzle. It depends on whether I've guessed right about what one person will do in a given set of circumstances." He added, "Which is always dangerous."

Moira Hastings was the first to arrive. She came at a quarter to eight. Under the brown beaver coat which she dropped to the chair by the door, she had on the gray dress she had worn a week before. Her manner was puzzling to Victoria. At first she wore a dignified hauteur which lapsed into little placating comments, and finally fell away into what seemed like simple nervousness. They sat at either end of the sofa in the living-room. "Do *you* know what this is all about?" Moira asked, turning toward Victoria.

"No. Tuck said he might be late."

"He told me to be here at eight," said Moira Hastings.

There was a silence. Neither of them, Victoria realized, could think of anything to say.

At 8:15 Victoria asked Moira if she'd like a drink. Moira said a little sherry would be nice. Victoria went to the bar and poured two glasses of the wine. As she walked down the dining-room she noticed that one of the French doors to the balcony was slightly ajar.

"Is this your maid's night off again, or did you fire her?" asked Moira as she took the sherry.

"Why would I fire her?"

Moira gave her a quick, sidewise glance and then looked

into her glass. "If she put the poison in the sugar bowl—" she said.

Victoria said, "I don't think Mr. Tuck likes that idea."

Moira stirred on the sofa. Victoria went to the radio beside the fireplace and turned it on. When she looked back at Moira she found the cold blue eyes looking at her.

The band whose music grew loud in the room was playing *Dardanella*. As Victoria sat down in the corner of the sofa she said, "That song always has a funny nostalgia for me. I heard it first when I was ten years old. On a phonograph with a big horn. It always brings me a hot New York summer in nineteen-eighteen."

"I wasn't born yet," said Moira.

Victoria drank the rest of her sherry. As she set the wineglass down on the coffee table, Moira said, "I didn't notice your ring when I saw you before. It's lovely. I've always liked sapphires."

"Albert bought it for my birthday."

Moira was slumped back against the sofa. At the words her eyes rose and searched Victoria's face, and then dropped to the ring again. "He did?" she asked. Her voice was scarcely audible.

*"Oh, sweet Dardanella,"* sang a man's voice, *"I love your harem eyes."*

Moira suddenly laughed. "What crazy words," she said. "Such a lovely tune and such crazy words!"

She stood up abruptly. She looked at her little gold wrist watch. She hummed along with the music. She went to the round mirror over the radio and looked at herself. She said suddenly, bitterly, "I'm so tired of things!" She turned and snapped the radio off. In the sudden silence that followed she stood looking across the width of the room at Victoria. "It's a lousy world! People aren't friends. They use each other, that's all."

She jerked her slim wrist up and looked again at her watch. "I don't like this. I wish it were over." She took a step toward Victoria and said, "It was an accident, after all. The old woman with the glasses made a mistake. It has to be that way. Because if you didn't kill him, and she didn't, how did he come to die?"

The doorbell rang violently.

Victoria walked down the dining-room, opened the top half of the door. Sawn was standing outside. He had on an officer's short overcoat. When she opened the lower half of the door to admit him, she saw the tan satchel in his right hand. He pulled off his cap, stuffed it into his pocket, looked around curiously.

"He's not here yet," she said tersely. "We're waiting in the living-room." They walked the length of the dining-room, on either side of the long table. His shoes made heavy sounds on the floor. He dropped his bag beside the sofa. "Miss Hastings, Captain Harriss," said Victoria. They inclined their heads and spoke the usual words.

Sawn turned to Victoria, rubbing his hands together. "I haven't much time," he said, "but I'll sweat it out awhile. How about a drink?"

Victoria turned to Moira. "Sherry?"

"No, thanks."

Victoria mixed Sawn a Scotch and soda. When she returned to the living-room, he and Moira Hastings were talking about Hollywood. He took the drink, and Victoria sat in the chair facing the two of them, half-listening to their voices rise and fall, but making no effort to take part in the talk. She was intensely aware of the queerness of the situation. She wondered when Bernice would come, when Tuck would arrive, and what would happen then.

She heard a scratching sound at the front door, and let Haggis in. Haggis bounced down the length of the living-room, sniffed Moira's slender ankles and fell in love with Sawn. As he leaned one arm down to scratch Haggis's head, Sawn looked up at Victoria and said, "Dogs always like me. Dogs and children."

The doorbell pealed again, and Victoria's heart bounded. But only a taxi driver was there, his peaked cap askew. "Cab for Captain Harriss," he said.

She turned and saw Sawn settling his cap on his dark head. He said, "Nice to have known you," to Moira. He picked up his satchel and walked toward Victoria, confidently.

"But you can't go!" she told him.

"Duty calls." His eyes were without expression.

"But Tuck isn't here yet!"

"Obviously." Sawn opened the lower half of the door. "Good-by, Victoria. I wish I could have been around for the end of the story."

He went out the door. He turned and said easily, "Thanks for the drink."

Desperation seized her, and the sense that something had gone wrong, completely wrong.

"I've told Tuck what I know," said Sawn. "I signed the deposition this afternoon, so he has my two bits' worth."

"He didn't tell me about any deposition!"

Sawn's eyebrows went up. "No? He will, then. This afternoon I swore to the fact that there was no poison in the lethal sugar bowl on the night your husband died."

She stared up at him.

"Sorry as hell, little friend. But it had to come out, you know."

Frozen, she watched him go down the steps behind the hurrying cabby. She heard the quick crunch of their footsteps on the gravel of the driveway. Dazedly, she turned in the doorway. She could feel the cold night coming in at her back. She knew that she had just heard the voice of a murderer, and that he had gone calmly away in a taxicab.

The growing suspicion of Sawn's abnormality which had been a shadowy, half-acknowledged matter was unbelievable now that it stood so sharply revealed. Victoria thought first of telephoning Tuck. Then she realized that he must already be on his way to her house. Dazedly, she closed the front door.

When she turned to go to the living-room, Moira was coming toward her. She was walking slowly; she was like a statue walking. She looked a little frightened.

Victoria went to the bar in the hall, poured and drank some brandy. Moira stood in the doorway watching her. When Victoria left the hall, Moira stood aside to let her pass.

Victoria found that her knees were weak. She went to the dining-table, pulled back Albert's chair, and sat down limply. She propped her hot forehead with cold hands. Moira's voice came from behind her. "There's one thing I'd like you to understand," Moira said. "There was nothing cheap about it—it wasn't the sort of thing you think it was. We were never lovers, really, the way most people use the word."

Victoria's brain stuck. She could hear Moira's words as though they were being played back to her. She raised her head, turned slowly in her chair to look at the other woman, who was standing straight and slim in her gray dress, excited eyes shining in her tense face.

"You're talking about yourself and Albert?" asked Victoria.

For some reason this seemed to make Moira Hastings angry. "Oh, come now!" she said, in a cool and supercilious little voice. "Let's not play games. I just wanted you to know how it was, in justice to myself." She walked gracefully to the other end of the table, apparently thinking deeply. She slid back the tall carved chair and sat down. The dark wood of the back of the chair threw her light and shining hair into bold relief. Her perfect breasts, like the breasts of a statue, jutted sharply forward under the brightness of the overhead light. Her arms rested along the arms of the chair. "I'm a virgin," said Moira Hastings.

Looking at Victoria down the dark length of the table, she continued: "I came here tonight feeling bad because of a lie I told the detective, a lie that went against you. I had to tell it. I got thinking that maybe you didn't kill him, that maybe it *was* an accident. It made me sick. And when I saw the ring, that upset me too. But now it's all right. Now it's clear. There wasn't any poison in the sugar until you put it there. There wasn't any accident. There couldn't have been."

"You're saying," Victoria said, "that I poisoned Albert because he was in love with you."

"Yes. But it wasn't what you think! It was a crazy thing, the way it happened to us. I met him through my agent. Right away I knew I could work on Albert. You get to know that, with a man. The ones who don't need you seem insulated. Albert needed some woman who would tell him how good he was. I wanted a good part. I've done that all my life, I guess. I never get on with women, but beginning with Daddy, I could always get things out of men. You build them up, looking up, listening, smiling and then, finally, there's something you ask them for. They can't refuse, because they don't want to lose you. It's never spoken in words, but they know that if they keep their side of the bargain, you'll keep on making them feel big.

"It began when I needed what Albert could do for me, and he needed what I did for him. And then it was different, all at once. It was wonderful. We saw each other whenever we could. He came past my place almost every afternoon. He told me from the first how fond he was of you. I didn't expect to see him nights. Not at first.

"But after four months of this we knew it wasn't any good. That there would have to be a divorce. He said he didn't want to hurt you. The night he died I told him he'd have to tell you. In the café. I wanted the part, too. That all got mixed into it. I told him things couldn't go on this way." She paused. "He refused to do anything then. Because of Leighman. Because Leighman liked you. Because if you were against Albert, he'd be too. And I told him that if he didn't finish it off with you, I was through."

Victoria saw with vague surprise that Moira Hastings's face was screwing up into a distorted grimace. Tears started into her eyes, slid out of the corners onto her cheeks. "But he told you he loved me and you killed him for it!" She leaned suddenly forward, her hands clawed on the ends of the chair arms. "You killed him!"

Victoria stood up. She heard her own voice speak with slow clarity. "No. He tried to kill me."

There was a slight clatter. Victoria turned toward the sound. Tuck had entered the room through the French doors leading onto the little balcony. He stood there, huge, backed by glass with the night behind it. She was surprised by his appearance, but that was a secondary feeling. In a strange voice Victoria said to him, "It was the coffee, not the sugar. He put the poison into my coffee just after Bernice telephoned. When he was on the telephone I heated that same coffee. I gave it to him."

Tuck was nodding. "Yes. That's how it was." His long head turned slowly and he looked down at Moira. "I am wondering whether to arrest you as accessory before the fact."

Moira shrank against the carving of the high-backed chair. "I didn't have anything to do with it!"

Victoria found that she felt almost sorry for the woman sitting opposite her. "It was all Albert, I think," she told Tuck.

As she spoke, Moira shot to her feet. "I don't believe it! It's only your word! You had as good a chance!" She turned sharply to Tuck, who was still standing on the balcony doorway.

Tuck shook his head.

Moira turned slowly and looked at Victoria. Then a brightness blossomed on her face. Her eyes were suddenly stars. Moving limpidly, gently, she eased away from the table. She moved gracefully to the chair by the door. She picked up her fur coat. With a sudden swirl, she swung it from her shoulders, like a cape. She drifted to the front door, which opened easily for her. She stood with her back to them, facing the night air. "I'll never get to do that part. You'll see to that. You'll have it your way. But I had him." She turned. She was very pretty, standing there. There was a sweetness on her face. Her voice was a sliver of ice. "How does it feel to know that he tried to kill you, for me?" She tipped the upper part of her body forward. One hand pointed inward at her breast. "For me!" she repeated.

"No," said Victoria. "For himself."

"He hated you!" said Moira. Her starry eyes were incongruous with the icy voice.

Victoria walked toward her across the space between them. There was something in that slow and quiet approach which made Moira draw back.

Facing Moira, Victoria said to her, "You don't understand Albert. Albert had only the kindliest feelings for women he had used."

A new look showed on Moira Hastings's face, a puzzled understanding. The strange, momentary beauty had left her now.

"When you cry into your pillow tonight, ask yourself how it would have gone if he had come to discover that *you* were the unnecessary one."

Moira's exit was not an exit after all.

*Chapter Fourteen:*
## DAYDREAM INTO REALITY

TUCK MADE coffee. He sat in the chair that was too small for him. They drank one cup in silence, and then he brought them each another. "Your plan worked," Victoria said. "You arranged it so Sawn would say what he did in front of Moira Hastings. You hoped she would tell what she told."

"Yes," said Tuck. "I needed her admission of that relationship with your husband. She gave me a little more than I'd counted on."

"What," asked Victoria, "did Albert see in her?"

"She told you that. He saw a face looking up, which made him taller. He saw eyes which said, 'You're wonderful.' He found relief from the sense of inadequacy you gave him. He'd begun to doubt himself. He needed what she gave him, needed it badly."

"I can't get used to it," Victoria said. "I know it happened, but I keep thinking of what I believed Albert to be, and I can't get used to it. He would have murdered me for nothing—to keep a pretty girl, to keep a chance to produce a picture."

Tuck nodded. "Yes. These were important enough to Albert."

"It makes him sound like a person with no sense, no sense at all!"

"He was mad with common sense," said Tuck. "A good many people are."

"But he certainly realized I wasn't desperately in love with him! That to learn about Moira wouldn't shatter my life!"

"Do you think he did it? I don't. He liked himself pretty well."

"Yes," said Victoria. "He did."

"I think he believed that to tell you about Moira would have only one result. After a harrowing scene, you would become angry and would at once try to ruin his chance with Leighman."

"He couldn't have!"

"And are you sure you wouldn't have done just that?"

Victoria stared at the long face opposite. She thought about herself. "I *might* have turned bitchy," she said.

The three tin masks were staring at her. She lowered her eyes from them and looked around the room. Albert had sat looking at this room before he put the poison in her coffee, and after. Anger stirred in her. Not at Albert—at herself. How had she been blind for so long? Not to the relationship between him and Moira. Her absorption in her own work made her one of the few wives who could remain oblivious to such a situation. It was her blindness about what Albert had been that angered her.

Albert's voice came back to her, the words he had spoken on the night she had agreed to marry him. "You would always give a man more than he expected . . ." And her own voice, "In other words, I'm a good deal." And Albert: "Yes, if you want to put it that way."

The candor of the man had fooled her. He saw people very simply. Like cards in a game—high cards, low cards. People were useful to him, or not useful. But this was no secret thing, no hidden malady. Believing everyone else to be like himself, he had been quite frank and open. And she had been unable to grasp the quiet monstrosity which had shown itself even before she became his wife.

Albert's maggot, she saw, was curiously without psychological undertones. It was plain, garden variety of self-engrossment carried to a final extreme.

Victoria picked up her coffee cup and with the other hand reached for a cigarette from the box on the table. She saw the blue ring shining on her left hand.

"Facts," said Tuck, "for which most people have such respect, are dangerous. The root of my confusion about this case lay in my interpretation of one fact. The chemist found poison in the sugar bowl. So I assumed that it had been the sugar in that bowl which killed your husband. That glaring mistake in my thinking was supported by the fact that he had been seen by you to use sugar from that bowl, at the time he must have taken the poison.

"One statement finally showed the poisoned sugar in its true light. Captain Harriss's statement that he had used sugar from that bowl at seven-thirty. It would have been better if he'd told me that as soon as he realized it, which was during a conversation between the two of you on your balcony. But he fooled around for a while with the idea that you had killed your husband, and kept quiet about what he felt would prove this to me. However, he had abandoned that idea by the time I questioned him about the sugar. When he signed the deposition, he told me you might shoot a man but would never poison him.

"So what he had to say about the sugar left the situation for the first time stripped bare. No one except yourself or your husband could have poisoned it. And by that time I was sure that Moira Hastings had lied, and why. And even before that, I had begun to suspect Hime."

"Before that?"

"When you showed me the ring he gave you and told me when he ordered it."

"Not until then?"

Tuck's face looked mournful. "Doesn't make me sound very bright, does it? But then, you had been married to him, and you didn't guess until Miss Hastings told her little story."

"Go on," said Victoria.

"A thought flashed into my head, from nowhere. Not a very logical thought, just the uneasy feeling that a husband who had forgotten his wife's birthday until the last moment had behaved oddly in wiring for a ring which could not arrive until a week afterward. He could have bought just as handsome a ring the next day at a jeweler's in Los Angeles or Hollywood. Why get up out of bed and order one from New York? A rather poetic notion occurred to me—that it was almost as though the man had somehow known he would be dead the next day. Then came the corollary of that idea: 'Or that he had known his wife would be dead.' While I stood looking at the ring on your finger, two crazy comments chased themselves around my brain. 'A corpse can't buy a ring. You don't buy a ring for a corpse.' It was when I realized why a man might buy a ring for a corpse that I saw the whole picture reversed. I saw you as the intended victim, not Albert."

Victoria looked down at the ring on her hand. She pulled it from her finger. She let it roll from her hand onto the coffee table. It came to rest with the heavy stone face down, the platinum hoop uppermost. "Of course," she said slowly. "An afterthought. He believed I had drunk poison. He had planted the poison in the sugar bowl. He intended that my death should pass as the result of Hazel's mistake. He was going to play the bereaved husband. And he had forgotten my birthday. So he decided to remember it."

Tuck nodded.

"And when did you learn about the coffee?"

"To put it chronologically, I knew from Captain Harriss's statement that only you or your husband could have poisoned the sugar. I also knew why he could have done so. Yet he used sugar from that bowl. Therefore it could not have contained poison at that time. Therefore it was never the means of administering the poison. What else? The coffee. And that's where the whole picture clarified.

"I tried to reconstruct that little dinner. The man at the head of the table, gnawed by his problem. His eyes falling perhaps on the green canisters which he could see through the open kitchen door. The sudden, flashing realization that with you dead he would have both Moira Hastings and the opportunity he wanted so intensely. The realization of the danger to himself. The recollection of the mistake Hazel had made when she put salt into the sugar bowl. The sugar bowl on the table before him. But you weren't using sugar. Your coffee cup, with the coffee poured out, waiting for you. Your voice on the telephone in the hall. He went to the kitchen for the poison. He stirred it into your coffee.

"After the dishes had been rinsed—I imagine he took especial care with your cup—you spent a quiet evening together, and went to your separate rooms. He was reminded of your birthday by the music next door. He got up, put the poison in the sugar and added the new flourish of wiring for the ring. He wrote a check—there was an inkstain on his finger the next day—and left the envelope out at the mailbox for the postman to pick up in the morning. He went back to bed. After a while he began to feel ill. The pain became really bad. He got up, started for the door to call you or telephone a doctor. He never got there."

Victoria said, "That was Albert. He never got there. He always fell just a little short of reaching what he wanted. Because he cheated, but he didn't know that." Her briefly philosophical mood left her suddenly. She leaned sharply toward Tuck. "But look!" she said loudly. "How will you ever prove that I didn't kill Albert? That I didn't put the poison into *his* coffee? His affair with Moira Hastings gives me a motive for killing him, if I were jealous! That leaves only the ring, and why he ordered it! Is that enough against him?"

Tuck sighed. "That," he said, "is the catch. The risk, I think, is too great. That's why this case is going to be one of my failures. Froody will know. He always knows. The papers will say death by accident, which is quite true."

Victoria looked at the ring on the table. "I'm glad," she said. She looked at Tuck and forced herself to say, "I'm full of cheap female pride. To have the whole world know what he did for that little blond thing would be unbearable."

Tuck said, "I will always think of him as a case history. As a perfect example of a pattern so universal that no one regards it as strange. The success pattern. The simple-hearted dedication of every act to the achievement of a private goal. The simple-hearted belief that any means justifies this end. When he was eighteen he married a woman who paid his way through college; after he had graduated he gracefully acceded to a divorce. His second marriage was to an heiress. She paid for his first Broadway production. After that, he was willing that she go, too. He found your brains could be useful to him, and he married you. The little actress was the first woman who was useful to him because she was herself. In a way that upset his applecart. For Albert Hime, that was love. Through the one woman he could not bear to lose, he lost his life. I suppose that might be called poetic justice."

The doorbell rang. "That, I think, will be your friend Mrs. Saxe," said Tuck. "I told her I did not think you should be alone tonight. I'll be getting along now."

As Bernice came into the house, Tuck left, his broad shoulders filling the doorway for a moment. Victoria watched him go down the steps to the driveway. Suddenly she recalled something that had puzzled her. "How did you get out there on my balcony?" she called.

With his hand on his car door Tuck looked up at her. "I climbed a tree," he said. He got into his black sedan.

Bernice wanted to know why Tuck had asked her to come. While they undressed for bed Victoria told her everything. Bernice was loud in her castigation of Albert, profuse in her sympathy. But her brown eyes shone brightly.

They lay side by side as they had so many times down the years. From the darkness Bernice suddenly spoke. "That hat," she said. "Do you suppose Hazel would like it?"

"What are you talking about?" asked Victoria.

"That pink hat. The one I bought for the inquest."

"You mean you went out and bought a hat especially for the inquest? *That* hat?"

"Certainly. It made me look like a fool, which is what I wanted. That made it quite believable to the coroner and the jury that I'd become hysterical and thrown the poison out for no reason at all. I didn't want anyone to know that I thought, for just a tiny while, that you could have killed Albert."

"Darling," said Victoria. "You are really wonderful."

There was another silence.

"I wonder when you'll learn to humor men," said Bernice. "You just have to humor them, Victoria. This whole thing happened, really, because you made Albert sleep in the guest room, and things like that."

"Go to sleep," said Victoria. "I don't want to talk about it any more."

There was a silence. "Men are just like boys," said Bernice, dreamily. "Just large children."

"Just large children, and full of pranks. Poison in the coffee, blondes in the shower."

"I keep thinking of Albert, sleeping in the guest room," repeated Bernice.

"I keep thinking of him dead in the guest room," said Victoria. "But then I'm a hard character. He told me so himself."

Two months after Albert's death Victoria was working in her den when the doorbell rang. It rang again and she realized that Hazel was at the market. Grumbling to herself, she ran down the hall and opened the door. Sawn was on the porch.

"First leave I've had," he said. "So I thought I'd drop in to see how things were by you."

He entered the house and looked about him. "I wasn't sure you'd be here. I thought you might have moved."

"Why would I move?" she asked, as they walked down to the living-room.

"Well," said Sawn, "unpleasant associations, you know."

"If I *had* rented this house and moved somewhere else, it wouldn't have altered the fact that Albert tried to kill me here," said Victoria.

"No," agreed Sawn cautiously.

"I'm working," said Victoria as they sat down on the sofa, "on a new story. But you can stay for a little while."

After they had lighted cigarettes she said, "It's really a won-

derful idea that I've got!" She felt her idea take possession of
her. She stood up, and began to walk it out, Sawn watching
from the sofa. She talked for twenty minutes, dropping ashes
until her cigarette was too short to smoke, at which point she
put it out in a small dish containing candy. She realized this
too late. The sapphire on her right hand flashed blue fire as she
gestured. "What do you think?" she asked at last.

"Sounds all right," said Sawn. "But there's something that
interests me more. That ring you're wearing. Didn't the departed Albert give you that?"

She looked at the gem on her hand. "Oh, yes."

"And yet you wear it." He shook his head from side to side.
"You puzzle me, little friend."

"There's no sadness to wearing it," she said. "When a gift
outlasts the sentiment that prompted it, that's sad. This ring
was given without sentiment. So I can wear it. It's a beautiful
ring. It's the most beautiful thing I've ever owned."

"I will never understand you," said Sawn. A slightly malicious look came over his face. "I take comfort in the fact
that you don't know me any better. All that dissertation
about my Don Juanism. I outgrew that years ago. And the
blonde in the shower—you were wrong about her, old girl."
He grinned. "In fact, for such a psychologically alert lassie,
you've shown yourself a little thick, you know. Your second
husband was actually guilty of what you suspected of me. You
never tumbled to it at all."

Victoria sat down, somewhat deflated. "You're right," she
said. "I didn't." She brightened. "But I knew Albert, in a way.
Because I knew what his daydream was. We all have day-

dreams we never tell. If you know what a person's daydream is, you know the essence of him. And I think I guessed Albert's."

She stood up again, and began to walk the room rather slowly. "Albert's daydream was on the end of the journey, the moment celebrating some final gain, after which he would be rich and happy. That moment went something like this: To a woman standing near a mirror in an elegant room containing *Louis Quinze* furniture, Albert would hand a black velvet box. The woman would open it and then gasp at a magnificent necklace. Albert would fasten the clasp while she stared with wonder at her reflection in the mirror. Albert would pour them each a large glass of champagne, and they would quaff it. Albert would light a dollar cigar with a ten-dollar bill and she would listen with adoration while he told her how he had been born poor on the streets of Chicago."

A new thought struck Victoria. She paused in the center of the room. She raised her hand, looked down at the sapphire ring. "How sad," she said aloud. "How very sad." She looked up at Sawn's watching face. "I think this ring is the only jewel he ever bought a woman."

Sawn asked softly, "And what is your daydream, Victoria?"

She shook her head. "That's something I never tell anyone."

Sawn repeated, "What's your daydream, Victoria?"

His brown eyes went to the ring on her hand. She put that hand behind her. "Or shall I tell you?" asked Sawn, softly. "Shall I tell you what your daydream is?"

Victoria looked at him and knew. "All right," she said. "To be the woman to whom the necklace is given."

Sawn bounded to his feet. "I was sure of it! I was sure that you were a woman somewhere inside! Really female, wanting what most of them do!"

"And to think," said Victoria, "that it took you only eleven years to find out!"

"There's time ahead," said Sawn.

THE END

# DISCUSSION QUESTIONS

- Did any aspects of the plot date the story? If so, which?

- Would the story be different if it were set in the present day? If so, how?

- Did the social context of the time play a role in the narrative? If so, how?

- What role did the setting play in the narrative?

- If you were one of the main characters, would you have acted differently at any point in the story?

- Did you identify with any of the characters? If so, which?

- What skills or qualities make Richard Tuck an effective sleuth?

- Did this book remind you of any present day authors? If so, which?

- Did anything about this book surprise you? If so, what?

**Charlotte Armstrong, *The Chocolate Cobweb*.** When Amanda Garth was born, a mix-up caused the hospital to briefly hand her over to the prestigious Garrison family instead of to her birth parents. The error was quickly fixed, Amanda was never told, and the secret was forgotten for twenty-three years … until her aunt revealed it in casual conversation. But what if the initial switch never actually occurred? **Introduction by A. J. Finn.**

**Charlotte Armstrong, *The Unsuspected*.** First published in 1946, this suspenseful novel opens with a young woman who has ostensibly hanged herself, leaving a suicide note. Her friend doesn't believe it and begins an investigation that puts her own life in jeopardy. It was filmed in 1947 by Warner Brothers, starring Claude Rains and Joan Caulfield. **Introduction by Otto Penzler.**

**Anthony Boucher, *The Case of the Baker Street Irregulars*.** When a studio announces a new hard-boiled Sherlock Holmes film, the Baker Street Irregulars begin a campaign to discredit it. Attempting to mollify them, the producers invite members to the set, where threats are received, each referring to one of the original Holmes tales, followed by murder. Fortunately, the amateur sleuths use Holmesian lessons to solve the crime. **Introduction by Otto Penzler.**

**Anthony Boucher, *Rocket to the Morgue*.** Hilary Foulkes has made so many enemies that it is difficult to speculate who was responsible for stabbing him nearly to death in a room with only one door through which no one was seen entering or leaving. This classic locked room mystery is populated by such thinly disguised science fiction legends as Robert Heinlein, L. Ron Hubbard, and John W. Campbell. **Introduction by F. Paul Wilson.**

**Fredric Brown, *The Fabulous Clipjoint*.** Brown's outstanding mystery won an Edgar as the best first novel of the year (1947). When Wallace

Hunter is found dead in an alley after a long night of drinking, the police don't really care. But his teenage son Ed and his uncle Am, the carnival worker, are convinced that some things don't add up and the crime isn't what it seems to be. **Introduction by Lawrence Block.**

**John Dickson Carr, *The Crooked Hinge*.** Selected by a group of mystery experts as one of the 15 best impossible crime novels ever written, this is one of Gideon Fell's greatest challenges. Estranged from his family for 25 years, Sir John Farnleigh returns to England from America to claim his inheritance but another person turns up claiming that he can prove he is the real Sir John. Inevitably, one of them is murdered. **Introduction by Charles Todd.**

**John Dickson Carr, *The Eight of Swords*.** When Gideon Fell arrives at a crime scene, it appears to be straightforward enough. A man has been shot to death in an unlocked room and the likely perpetrator was a recent visitor. But Fell discovers inconsistencies and his investigations are complicated by an apparent poltergeist, some American gangsters, and two meddling amateur sleuths. **Introduction by Otto Penzler.**

**John Dickson Carr, *The Mad Hatter Mystery*.** A prankster has been stealing top hats all around London. Gideon Fell suspects that the same person may be responsible for the theft of a manuscript of a long-lost story by Edgar Allan Poe. The hats reappear in unexpected but conspicuous places but, when one is found on the head of a corpse by the Tower of London, it is evident that the thefts are more than pranks. **Introduction by Otto Penzler.**

**John Dickson Carr, *The Plague Court Murders*.** When murder occurs in a locked hut on Plague Court, an estate haunted by the ghost of a hangman's assistant who died a victim of the black death, Sir Henry Merrivale seeks a logical solution to a ghostly crime. A spiritual medium employed to rid the house of his spirit is found stabbed to death in a locked stone hut on the grounds, surrounded by an untouched circle of mud. **Introduction by Michael Dirda.**

**John Dickson Carr, *The Red Widow Murders*.** In a "haunted" mansion, the room known as the Red Widow's Chamber proves lethal to all who spend the night. Eight people investigate and the one who draws the ace of spades must sleep in it. The room is locked from the inside and watched all night by the others. When the door is unlocked, the victim has been poisoned. Enter Sir Henry Merrivale to solve the crime. **Introduction by Tom Mead.**

**Frances Crane, *The Turquoise Shop*.** In an arty little New Mexico town, Mona Brandon has arrived from the East and becomes the subject of gossip about her money, her influence, and the corpse in the nearby desert who may be her husband. Pat Holly, who runs the local gift shop, is as interested as anyone in the goings on—but even more in Pat Abbott, the detective investigating the possible murder. **Introduction by Anne Hillerman.**

**Todd Downing, *Vultures in the Sky*.** There is no end to the series of terrifying events that befall a luxury train bound for Mexico. First, a man dies when the train passes through a dark tunnel, then it comes to an abrupt stop in the middle of the desert. More deaths occur when night falls and the passengers panic when they realize they are trapped with a murderer on the loose. **Introduction by James Sallis.**

**Mignon G. Eberhart, *Murder by an Aristocrat*.** Nurse Keate is called to help a man who has been "accidentally" shot in the shoulder. When he is murdered while convalescing, it is clear that there was no accident. Although a killer is loose in the mansion, the family seems more concerned that news of the murder will leave their circle. *The New Yorker* wrote than "Eberhart can weave an almost flawless mystery." **Introduction by Nancy Pickard.**

**Erle Stanley Gardner, *The Case of the Baited Hook*.** Perry Mason gets a phone call in the middle of the night and his potential client says it's urgent, that he has two one-thousand-dollar bills that he will give him as a retainer, with an additional ten-thousand whenever he is called on to represent him. When

Mason takes the case, it is not for the caller but for a beautiful woman whose identity is hidden behind a mask. **Introduction by Otto Penzler.**

**Erle Stanley Gardner, *The Case of the Borrowed Brunette*.** A mysterious man named Mr. Hines has advertised a job for a woman who has to fulfill very specific physical requirements. Eva Martell, pretty but struggling in her career as a model, takes the job but her aunt smells a rat and hires Perry Mason to investigate. Her fears are realized when Hines turns up in the apartment with a bullet hole in his head. **Introduction by Otto Penzler.**

**Erle Stanley Gardner, *The Case of the Careless Kitten*.** Helen Kendal receives a mysterious phone call from her vanished uncle Franklin, long presumed dead, who urges her to contact Perry Mason. Soon, she finds herself the main suspect in the murder of an unfamiliar man. Her kitten has just survived a poisoning attempt—as has her aunt Matilda. What is the connection between Franklin's return and the murder attempts? **Introduction by Otto Penzler.**

**Erle Stanley Gardner, *The Case of the Rolling Bones*.** One of Gardner's most successful Perry Mason novels opens with a clear case of blackmail, though the person being blackmailed claims he isn't. It is not long before the police are searching for someone wanted for killing the same man in two different states—thirty-three years apart. The confounding puzzle of what happened to the dead man's toes is a challenge. **Introduction by Otto Penzler.**

**Erle Stanley Gardner, *The Case of the Shoplifter's Shoe*.** Most cases for Perry Mason involve murder but here he is hired because a young woman fears her aunt is a kleptomaniac. Sarah may not have been precisely the best guardian for a collection of valuable diamonds and, sure enough, they go missing. When the jeweler is found shot dead, Sarah is spotted leaving the murder scene with a bundle of gems stuffed in her purse. **Introduction by Otto Penzler.**

**Erle Stanley Gardner, *The Bigger They Come*.** Gardner's first novel using the pseudonym A.A. Fair starts off a series featuring the large and loud Bertha Cool and her employee, the small and meek Donald Lam. Given the job of delivering divorce papers to an evident crook,

Lam can't find him—but neither can the police. The *Los Angeles Times* called this book: "Breathlessly dramatic ... an original." **Introduction by Otto Penzler.**

**Frances Noyes Hart, *The Bellamy Trial*.** Inspired by the real-life Hall-Mills case, the most sensational trial of its day, this is the story of Stephen Bellamy and Susan Ives, accused of murdering Bellamy's wife Madeleine. Eight days of dynamic testimony, some true, some not, make headlines for an enthralled public. Rex Stout called this historic courtroom thriller one of the ten best mysteries of all time. **Introduction by Hank Phillippi Ryan.**

**H.F. Heard, *A Taste for Honey*.** The elderly Mr. Mycroft quietly keeps bees in Sussex, where he is approached by the reclusive and somewhat misanthropic Mr. Silchester, whose honey supplier was found dead, stung to death by her bees. Mycroft, who shares many traits with Sherlock Holmes, sets out to find the vicious killer. Rex Stout described it as "sinister ... a tale well and truly told." **Introduction by Otto Penzler.**

**Dolores Hitchens, *The Alarm of the Black Cat*.** Detective fiction aficionado Rachel Murdock has a peculiar meeting with a little girl and a dead toad, sparking her curiosity about a love triangle that has sparked anger. When the girl's great grandmother is found dead, Rachel and her cat Samantha work with a friend in the Los Angeles Police Department to get to the bottom of things. **Introduction by David Handler.**

**Dolores Hitchens, *The Cat Saw Murder*.** Miss Rachel Murdock, the highly intelligent 70-year-old amateur sleuth, is not entirely heartbroken when her slovenly, unattractive, bridge-cheating niece is murdered. Miss Rachel is happy to help the socially maladroit and somewhat bumbling Detective Lieutenant Stephen Mayhew, retaining her composure when a second brutal murder occurs. **Introduction by Joyce Carol Oates.**

**Dorothy B. Hughes, *Dread Journey*.** A bigshot Hollywood producer has worked on his magnum opus for years, hiring and firing one beautiful starlet after another. But Kitten Agnew's contract won't allow her to be fired, so she fears she might be terminated more permanently. Together with the producer on a train journey from Hollywood to Chicago, Kitten becomes more terrified with each passing mile. **Introduction by Sarah Weinman.**

**Dorothy B. Hughes, *Ride the Pink Horse*.** When Sailor met Willis Douglass, he was just a poor kid who Douglass groomed to work as a confidential secretary. As the senator became increasingly corrupt, he knew he could count on Sailor to clean up his messes. No longer a senator, Douglass flees Chicago for Santa Fe, leaving behind a murder rap and Sailor as the prime suspect. Seeking vengeance, Sailor follows. **Introduction by Sara Paretsky.**

**Dorothy B. Hughes, *The So Blue Marble*.** Set in the glamorous world of New York high society, this novel became a suspense classic as twins from Europe try to steal a rare and beautiful gem owned by an aristocrat whose sister is an even more menacing presence. *The New Yorker* called it "Extraordinary ... [Hughes'] brilliant descriptive powers make and unmake reality." **Introduction by Otto Penzler.**

**W. Bolingbroke Johnson, *The Widening Stain*.** After a cocktail party, the attractive Lucie Coindreau, a "black-eyed, black-haired Frenchwoman" visits the rare books wing of the library and apparently takes a headfirst fall from an upper gallery. Dismissed as a horrible accident, it seems dubious when Professor Hyett is strangled while reading a priceless 12th-century manuscript, which has gone missing. **Introduction by Nicholas A. Basbanes**

**Baynard Kendrick, *Blind Man's Bluff*.** Blinded in World War II, Duncan Maclain forms a successful private detective agency, aided by his two dogs. Here, he is called on to solve the case of a blind man who plummets from the top of an eight-story building, apparently with no one present except his dead-drunk son. **Introduction by Otto Penzler.**

**Baynard Kendrick, *The Odor of Violets*.** Duncan Maclain, a blind former intelligence officer, is asked to investigate the murder of an actor in his Greenwich Village apartment. This would cause a stir at any time but, when the actor possesses secret government plans that then go missing, it's enough to interest the local police as well as the American government and Maclain, who suspects a German spy plot. **Introduction by Otto Penzler.**

C. Daly King, *Obelists at Sea*. On a cruise ship traveling from New York to Paris, the lights of the smoking room briefly go out, a gunshot crashes through the night, and a man is dead. Two detectives are on board but so are four psychiatrists who believe their professional knowledge can solve the case by understanding the psyche of the killer—each with a different theory. **Introduction by Martin Edwards.**

**Jonathan Latimer, *Headed for a Hearse.*** Featuring Bill Crane, the booze-soaked Chicago private detective, this humorous hard-boiled novel was filmed as *The Westland Case* in 1937 starring Preston Foster. Robert Westland has been framed for the grisly murder of his wife in a room with doors and windows locked from the inside. As the day of his execution nears, he relies on Crane to find the real murderer. **Introduction by Max Allan Collins**

**Lange Lewis, *The Birthday Murder.*** Victoria is a successful novelist and screenwriter and her husband is a movie director so their marriage seems almost too good to be true. Then, on her birthday, her happy new life comes crashing down when her husband is murdered using a method of poisoning that was described in one of her books. She quickly becomes the leading suspect. **Introduction by Randal S. Brandt.**

**Frances and Richard Lockridge, *Death on the Aisle.*** In one of the most beloved books to feature Mr. and Mrs. North, the body of a wealthy backer of a play is found dead in a seat of the 45th Street Theater. Pam is thrilled to engage in her favorite pastime—playing amateur sleuth—much to the annoyance of Jerry, her publisher husband. The Norths inspired a stage play, a film, and long-running radio and TV series. **Introduction by Otto Penzler.**

**John P. Marquand, *Your Turn, Mr. Moto.*** The first novel about Mr. Moto, originally titled *No Hero*, is the story of a World War I hero pilot who finds himself jobless during the Depression. In Tokyo for a big opportunity that falls apart, he meets a Japanese agent and his Russian colleague and the pilot suddenly finds himself caught in a web of intrigue. Peter Lorre played Mr. Moto in a series of popular films. **Introduction by Lawrence Block.**

**Stuart Palmer, *The Penguin Pool Murder.*** The first adventure of schoolteacher and dedicated amateur sleuth Hildegarde Withers occurs at the New York Aquarium when she and her young students notice a corpse in one of the tanks. It was published in 1931 and filmed the next year, starring Edna May Oliver as the American Miss Marple—though much funnier than her English counterpart. **Introduction by Otto Penzler.**

**Stuart Palmer, *The Puzzle of the Happy Hooligan.*** New York City schoolteacher Hildegarde Withers cannot resist "assisting" homicide detective Oliver Piper. In this novel, she is on vacation in Hollywood and on the set of a movie about Lizzie Borden when the screenwriter is found dead. Six comic films about Withers appeared in the 1930s, most successfully starring Edna May Oliver. **Introduction by Otto Penzler.**

**Otto Penzler, ed., *Golden Age Bibliomysteries.*** Stories of murder, theft, and suspense occur with alarming regularity in the unlikely world of books and bibliophiles, including bookshops, libraries, and private rare book collections, written by such giants of the mystery genre as Ellery Queen, Cornell Woolrich, Lawrence G. Blochman, Vincent Starrett, and Anthony Boucher. **Introduction by Otto Penzler.**

**Otto Penzler, ed., *Golden Age Detective Stories.*** The history of American mystery fiction has its pantheon of authors who have influenced and entertained readers for nearly a century, reaching its peak during the Golden Age, and this collection pays homage to the work of the most acclaimed: Cornell Woolrich, Erle Stanley Gardner, Craig Rice, Ellery Queen, Dorothy B. Hughes, Mary Roberts Rinehart, and more. **Introduction by Otto Penzler.**

**Otto Penzler, ed., *Golden Age Locked Room Mysteries.*** The so-called impossible crime category reached its zenith during the 1920s, 1930s, and 1940s, and this volume includes the greatest of the great authors who mastered the form: John Dickson Carr, Ellery Queen, C. Daly King, Clayton Rawson, and Erle Stanley Gardner. Like great magicians, these literary conjurors will baffle and delight readers. **Introduction by Otto Penzler.**

**Ellery Queen, *The Adventures of Ellery Queen.*** These stories are the earliest short works to feature Queen as a detective and are among the best of the author's fair-play mysteries. So many of the elements that comprise the gestalt of Queen may be found in these tales: alternate solutions, the dying clue, a bizarre crime, and the author's ability to find fresh variations of works by other authors. **Introduction by Otto Penzler.**

**Ellery Queen, *The American Gun Mystery.*** A rodeo comes to New York City at the Colosseum. The headliner is Buck Horne, the once popular film cowboy who opens the show leading a charge of forty whooping cowboys until they pull out their guns and fire into the air. Buck falls to the ground, shot dead. The police instantly lock the doors to search everyone but the offending weapon has completely vanished. **Introduction by Otto Penzler.**

**Ellery Queen, *The Chinese Orange Mystery.*** The offices of publisher Donald Kirk have seen strange events but nothing like this. A strange man is found dead with two long spears alongside his back. And, though no one was seen entering or leaving the room, everything has been turned backwards or upside down: pictures face the wall, the victim's clothes are worn backwards, the rug upside down. Why in the world? **Introduction by Otto Penzler.**

**Ellery Queen, *The Dutch Shoe Mystery.*** Millionaire philanthropist Abagail Doorn falls into a coma and she is rushed to the hospital she funds for an emergency operation by one of the leading surgeons on the East Coast. When she is wheeled into the operating theater, the sheet covering her body is pulled back to reveal her garroted corpse—the first of a series of murders **Introduction by Otto Penzler.**

**Ellery Queen, *The Egyptian Cross Mystery.*** A small-town schoolteacher is found dead, headed, and tied to a T-shaped cross on December 25th, inspiring such sensational headlines as "Crucifixion on Christmas Day." Amateur sleuth Ellery Queen is so intrigued he travels to Virginia but fails to solve the crime. Then a similar murder takes place on New York's Long Island—and then another. **Introduction by Otto Penzler.**

**Ellery Queen, *The Siamese Twin Mystery.*** When Ellery and his father encounter a raging forest fire on a mountain, their only hope is to drive up to an isolated hillside manor

owned by a secretive surgeon and his strange guests. While playing solitaire in the middle of the night, the doctor is shot. The only clue is a torn playing card. Suspects include a society beauty, a valet, and conjoined twins. **Introduction by Otto Penzler.**

**Ellery Queen, *The Spanish Cape Mystery.*** Amateur detective Ellery Queen arrives in the resort town of Spanish Cape soon after a young woman and her uncle are abducted by a gun-toting, one-eyed giant. The next day, the woman's somewhat dicey boyfriend is found murdered—totally naked under a black fedora and opera cloak. **Introduction by Otto Penzler.**

**Patrick Quentin, *A Puzzle for Fools.*** Broadway producer Peter Duluth takes to the bottle when his wife dies but enters a sanitarium to dry out. Malevolent events plague the hospital, including when Peter hears his own voice intone, "There will be murder." And there is. He investigates, aided by a young woman who is also a patient. This is the first of nine mysteries featuring Peter and Iris Duluth. **Introduction by Otto Penzler.**

**Clayton Rawson, *Death from a Top Hat.*** When the New York City Police Department is baffled by an apparently impossible crime, they call on The Great Merlini, a retired stage magician who now runs a Times Square magic shop. In his first case, two occultists have been murdered in a room locked from the inside, their bodies positioned to form a pentagram. **Introduction by Otto Penzler.**

**Craig Rice, *Eight Faces at Three.*** Gin-soaked John J. Malone, defender of the guilty, is notorious for getting his culpable clients off. It's the innocent ones who are problems. Like Holly Inglehart, accused of piercing the black heart of her well-heeled aunt Alexandria with a lovely Florentine paper cutter. No one knew the old battle-ax liked her, but Holly's prints were found on the murder weapon. **Introduction by Lisa Lutz.**

**Craig Rice, *Home Sweet Homicide.*** Known as the Dorothy Parker of mystery fiction for her memorable wit, Craig Rice was the first detective writer to appear on the cover of *Time* magazine. This comic mystery features two kids who are trying to find a husband for their widowed mother while she's engaged in sleuthing. Filmed with the same title in 1946 with Peggy Ann Garner and Randolph Scott. Introduction by Otto Penzler.

**Mary Roberts Rinehart, *The Album*.** Crescent Place is a quiet enclave of wealthy people in which nothing ever happens—until a bedridden old woman is attacked by an intruder with an ax. *The New York Times* stated: "All Mary Roberts Rinehart mystery stories are good, but this one is better." Introduction by Otto Penzler.

**Mary Roberts Rinehart, *The Haunted Lady*.** The arsenic in her sugar bowl was wealthy widow Eliza Fairbanks' first clue that somebody wanted her dead. Nightly visits of bats, birds, and rats, obviously aimed at scaring the dowager to death, was the second. Eliza calls the police, who send nurse Hilda Adams, the amateur sleuth they refer to as "Miss Pinkerton," to work undercover to discover the culprit. Introduction by Otto Penzler.

**Mary Roberts Rinehart, *Miss Pinkerton*.** Hilda Adams is a nurse, not a detective, but she is observant and smart and so it is common for Inspector Patton to call on her for help. Her success results in his calling her "Miss Pinkerton." *The New Republic* wrote: "From thousands of hearts and homes the cry will go up: Thank God for Mary Roberts Rinehart." Introduction by Carolyn Hart.

**Mary Roberts Rinehart, *The Red Lamp*.** Professor William Porter refuses to believe that the seaside manor he's just inherited is haunted but he has to convince his wife to move in. However, he soon sees evidence of the occult phenomena of which the townspeople speak. Whether it is a spirit or a human being, Porter accepts that there is a connection to the rash of murders that have terrorized the countryside. Introduction by Otto Penzler.

**Mary Roberts Rinehart, *The Wall*.** For two decades, Mary Roberts Rinehart was the second-best-selling author in America (only Sinclair Lewis outsold her) and was beloved for her tales of suspense. In a magnificent mansion, the ex-wife of one of the owners turns up making demands and is found dead the next day. And there are more dark secrets lying behind the walls of the estate. Introduction by Otto Penzler.

**Joel Townsley Rogers, *The Red Right Hand*.** This extraordinary whodunnit that is as puzzling as it is terrifying was identified by crime fiction scholar Jack Adrian as "one of the dozen or so finest mystery novels of the 20th century." A deranged killer sends a doctor on a quest for the truth—deep into the recesses of his own mind—when he and his bride-to-be elope but pick up a terrifying sharp-toothed hitch-hiker. Introduction by Joe R. Lansdale.

**Roger Scarlett, *Cat's Paw*.** The family of the wealthy old bachelor Martin Greenough cares far more about his money than they do about him. For his birthday, he invites all his potential heirs to his mansion to tell them what they hope to hear. Before he can disburse funds, however, he is murdered, and the Boston Police Department's big problem is that there are too many suspects. Introduction by Curtis Evans

**Vincent Starrett, *Dead Man Inside*.** 1930s Chicago is a tough town but some crimes are more bizarre than others. Customers arrive at a haberdasher to find a corpse in the window and a sign on the door: *Dead Man Inside! I am Dead. The store will not open today.* This is just one of a series of odd murders that terrorizes the city. Reluctant detective Walter Ghost leaps into action to learn what is behind the plague. Introduction by Otto Penzler.

**Vincent Starrett, *The Great Hotel Murder*.** Theater critic and amateur sleuth Riley Blackwood investigates a murder in a Chicago hotel where the dead man had changed rooms with a stranger who had registered under a fake name. *The New York Times* described it as "an ingenious plot with enough complications to keep the reader guessing." Introduction by Lyndsay Faye.

**Vincent Starrett, *Murder on 'B' Deck*.** Walter Ghost, a psychologist, scientist, explorer, and former intelligence officer, is on a cruise ship and his friend novelist Dunsten Mollock, a Nigel Bruce-like Watson whose role is to offer occasional comic relief, accommodates when he fails to leave the ship before it takes off. Although they make mistakes along the way, the amateur sleuths solve the shipboard murders. Introduction by Ray Betzner.

**Phoebe Atwood Taylor, *The Cape Cod Mystery*.** Vacationers have flocked to Cape Cod to avoid the heat wave that hit the Northeast and find their holiday unpleasant when the area is flooded with police trying to find the murderer of a muckraking journalist who took a cottage for the season. Finding a solution falls to Asey Mayo, "the Cape Cod Sherlock," known for his worldly wisdom, folksy humor, and common sense. **Introduction by Otto Penzler.**

**S. S. Van Dine,** *The Benson Murder Case.* The first of 12 novels to feature Philo Vance, the most popular and influential detective character of the early part of the 20th century. When wealthy stockbroker Alvin Benson is found shot to death in a locked room in his mansion, the police are baffled until the erudite flaneur and art collector arrives on the scene. Paramount filmed it in 1930 with William Powell as Vance. **Introduction by Ragnar Jónasson.**

**Cornell Woolrich,** *The Bride Wore Black.* The first suspense novel by one of the greatest of all noir authors opens with a bride and her new husband walking out of the church. A car speeds by, shots ring out, and he falls dead at her feet. Determined to avenge his death, she tracks down everyone in the car, concluding with a shocking surprise. It was filmed by Francois Truffaut in 1968, starring Jeanne Moreau. **Introduction by Eddie Muller.**

**Cornell Woolrich,** *Deadline at Dawn.* Quinn is overcome with guilt about having robbed a stranger's home. He meets Bricky, a dime-a-dance girl, and they fall for each other. When they return to the crime scene, they discover a dead body. Knowing Quinn will be accused of the crime, they race to find the true killer before he's arrested. A 1946 film starring Susan Hayward was loosely based on the plot. **Introduction by David Gordon.**

**Cornell Woolrich,** *Waltz into Darkness.* A New Orleans businessman successfully courts a woman through the mail but he is shocked to find when she arrives that she is not the plain brunette whose picture he'd received but a radiant blond beauty. She soon absconds with his fortune. Wracked with disappointment and loneliness, he vows to track her down. When he finds her, the real nightmare begins. **Introduction by Wallace Stroby.**